MW01254607

Music in the Air

Edited & Designed

by

Whitney Scott

Outrider Press

Music in the Air is published by
Outrider Press in affiliation with
TallGrass Writers Guild.

Book Design & Production
by
Whitney Scott

Susan Chiavelli's "Maybe It Happened This
Way" originally appeared in *Other Voices*, 2004.

Charles Fishman's "Listening to Brahms"
initially appeared in *Hawaii Review*, 1992.

Maureen Tolman Flannery's "Flower
Mountain Festival" was initially published
in *Atlanta Review*, 2007.

Sylvia Forges-Ryan's "The Guitarist Playing
Villa-Lobos" was originally published in
Sensations Magazine, 2004.

Pat Gallant's "Piano Solo" first appeared in
Christmas Traditions, Adams Media F & W
Publications, 2009

Allan Johnston's "heard singing" was originally
published in *Verdad*, Fall 2011.

Terry Martin's "Here on the Edge" originally
appeared in *Spindrift*, 2012.

Susanne Schuerman's "Early Morning
Concerto" first appeared in *True Words from Real
Women*, October 2011.

Julie Kim Shavin's "Prairie Song" was first
published in Of Mortality a Music,
DreamZion Press, 2011

Ingrid Swanberg's "summer's turn" appeared
in *Blueline*, Vol. 30, 2009, and in *Suzuki Grass*, Black
Rabbit Press, 2010

Dianalee Velie's "Orphean Aria" appeared in
Half Tones to Jubilee, Fall 2000, and *Glass Houses*, 2004;
Velie's "Claire de Lune" was originally
published in *The Many Roads to Paradise*, 2006.

Joseph Weintraub's "Performances" was first
published in *One Small Step*, Icarus, 2002

© 2013, Outrider Press
ISBN: 978-0-9851768-0-8
Outrider Press
2036 North Winds Drive
Dyer, IN 46311

Portions of this book made possible by a grant
from Illinois Arts Council

Dedicated to all who march to their own music

Contents

Poetry

Prose

⋮

10

⋮

Van Gogh's Ear

Martin Altman

Earless prophet, I
Heard Oedipus wail
As he gouged out his eyes,
Not seeing nor seen,
Not hearing nor heard,
Disappearing into a black dot.

Image in absentia,
Grasping for the fleshly lobe.
I stared at my ghostly presence.

Light cut me into fragments,
And scattered to the deaf and blind.
I'm a voice that grows through hand and eye,
No matter how I try to smother it.

When we dead awaken without eyes,
We will see like raindrops see the sky.
Without ears we will hear
Like roots that grow and die.
To have no ears
Yet hear the music of the spheres.

⋮

12

⋮

Music Appreciation Lesson

Susan Baller-Shepard

"It is not down in any map; true places never are." - Herman Melville

"When I hear music, I fear no danger. I am invulnerable. I see no foe. I am related to the earliest times, and to the latest." - Henry David Thoreau

As the sun rises, I take my oldest child Alex to school for marching band practice. Listening to Yo Yo Ma playing Ennio Morricone's music, we ride over yellow rural roads, yellow with the sun rising, yellow with the goldenrod in bloom, yellow with the reflection of dried corn. We listen to this piercing cello, Yo Yo's bow shreds the ordinary and makes this golden moment extraordinary.

Alex plays the clarinet. He also plays bass clarinet, tenor sax, piano, and drums. He's a gifted musician, and after only months of playing the sax, he was doing improv solos. He doesn't talk about this, he talks about sports: the ones he plays, the one he wishes he were playing (football), and the ones he watches on TV.

In sixth grade, after a month of playing violin, the orchestra teacher told me it would be "a waste of time" for me to continue, but that did not squelch my love of music.

Alex reaches to turn off Yo Yo for something else and I stop him. "Leave it. Listen," I say.

He looks out the window. "I can feel music," he says.

"I know you can," I say. How does someone come up with this? I ask, "How do you have this music in your head?"

Alex is fifteen, his friends are all driving now, and he will get his license soon. One of his friends is already notorious for not stopping at stop signs. Alex has grown eight inches in two years. I look up to him through that double vision parents possess, which sees both the curls on the adoring toddler and the man-child before me.

I wanted children more than I wanted air. When I became pregnant with Alex, I remember I drank iced tea one lunch, a wild move for me, as if to say, "See, I'd never drink caffeine if I really were pregnant." We'd had too many false starts. I didn't think it could be real. I felt too good. I told myself I was going to ace this motherhood thing. It was what I wanted most, and by God, I was going to do it well.

But nobody told me about the grief inherent in this parenting gig. Or maybe it's like people saying, "With infants, you get no sleep," and it seems spoken in another language until you actually have a newborn in your arms, and you can translate those words because you have gone so many nights without continuous sleep. Suddenly, I looked around, and my sons were emptying their rooms of all toys, and we had become serfs in the land of Electronica, where Technology rules, and everything has a charger. My ruling days were clearly over.

With Alex as my oldest child, I search for things to bond over. It's mostly music and food. I made him listen to Kings of Leon before they were popular, and told him for years about the genius of Andre Benjamin. Since Alex is hungry all the time, I buy or make mountains of food, he eats, and we are briefly, euphorically happy.

Since we live on the outskirts of town, there is only a Freedom gas station within biking distance, which, much to my chagrin, supplies my older two kids with caffeinated drinks, junk food, and God only knows what else. When Alex bikes over there with his friends, he yells out the door, "I'm going to Freedom." I have always found that shout out funny until now. Now it feels poignant.

"Wear your helmet. Be careful. Home before dark," I call out, in short, imperative sentences, as if teenagers remember these things, when racing toward Freedom.

I keep the poet Rilke close, always. I read this opening stanza:

As once the winged energy of delight
carried you over childhood's dark abysses,
now beyond your own life build the great
arch of unimagined bridges.

My own childhood's dark abysses left me vigilant about my children's childhoods. I do not want them left bereft. Traversing those abysses forged my courage, and sensitivity to art. Many things can bring me to tears, like this cello music as the sun is rising. My heart is full. My children are part of that great arch in my life; they themselves have been unimagined bridges.

As I drive, Alex looks at the cup holder and gear shift that separate us. It contains my coffee cup, a brown half-eaten banana, an empty pop bottle, some CD cases, and a protein bar wrapper.

"Good thing your car is so clean. I hope I keep the car as clean as you do," he says as he exits. I've been coached what I can say. I cannot embarrass him or sound too perky, so I simply say, "Have a good day." It doesn't begin to cover what I want to say to him. I want to tell him he and his siblings are the most beautiful people I have ever seen, how I have memorized the looks in his eyes and know the emotions they carry, how I know the way the back of his head looks as he turns away, how I memorized him as a baby in my arms, and how, since he's a moving target these days, I work to memorize him now.

Driving back home alone, I continue listening to Yo Yo Ma. I feel the music. His slow bow across the strings chokes me up. I remember when Alex learned Carl P. E. Bach's "Solfeggietto." His piano teacher, Robert Nakea, told me he'd never had a student learn the piece so quickly, as Alex's fingers went racing through the arpeggios. Robert told me, "It's a piece that takes time to learn. It's slow going at first, and then, voilà, it's learned, and if played well, it's a lot of work, but it's beautiful, and it speeds by." Just like parenthood.

⋮

16

⋮

The Best Seat in the House

Harker Brautighan

We have the dot-com boom to blame for a lot of things. Do I dare add loneliness to the list? Remember how the dot com-ers were always talking on their cell phones, typing into their PalmPilots and checking their pagers at the same time? And now, people can achieve the same amount of isolation and mind-numbing multitasking on their smart phones. And all the while a throbbing human heart is standing right in front of them. Everywhere you go you see throngs of people standing around, glued to their smartphones and ignoring each other. Someone asked me for the time last week. It was a small lance of interaction that pricked my otherwise solitary moment. That he didn't check his cell phone struck me as odd. That I checked not a cell phone, but a watch, was odd as well. I actually hadn't worn a watch since I got my first cell phone. Turns out, time pieces are the modern translation of the traditional paper anniversary present, so I got a watch for my first wedding anniversary a few months ago. I enjoyed being asked what time it was. Is this what our society has come to? That the only time a stranger speaks to you is when she sees the watch on your wrist? I look around waiting rooms and buses and college campuses and I see so many people so far apart. This culture of loneliness has permeated everywhere. Ironically, the more people isolate themselves with their phones, the less they know how to hold back the floodgates when they do interact with real people. I blame our ever-deteriorating fluency in social etiquette on loneliness.

I saw The Who in concert last Friday. Instead of just the usual talking I'll never get used to, I had to deal with the distraction of people arguing over how to use their smartphones to video the concert.

"Just go to Camera Roll and click this button," the lady two seats away from me shouted into her husband's ear. The discussion went on and on. The Who were playing "5:15" from *Quadrophenia*. I, too, thought I was going "out of my brain." When you're louder than The Who, you're effing loud. They play so loudly that the first time I saw them I was deaf for two days afterward. The voices I could hear sounded like Donald Duck's.

From the genius who was instructing her husband on the use of his phone I learned that The Who's drummer, John Bonham, had died; that John Entwistle, also dead, was their lead guitarist; and Simon Townshend was Pete Townshend's son. For those of you who don't know your Who trivia, John Bonham was with Led Zeppelin—The Who's deceased drummer is Keith Moon. John Entwistle played bass (Pete Townshend is known as one of the best guitarists in rock) and Simon Townshend is Pete's brother. The Who's current drummer, Zak Starkey, is Ringo Starr's son. And, by the way, if you want to take a video, why would you go to Camera Roll instead of just hitting the Camera button on your smartphone?

In addition to blabbing about cell phones, the concertgoers used their smartphones to text and update their Facebook pages. I used mine to take notes for this essay and to write notes to my husband. Like, duh, people. You can use your phones to be silent and courteous if you really need to communicate.

But this brings me back to loneliness.

Do people really *need* to communicate *during* a concert or a ballet or an opera? The empirical evidence seems to point to yes, but why is that? And why is nobody in tune enough to see the truth? Oh, I have heard others blame today's technology for loneliness. I'm not the first to think of it. But can't the talkers see it, too?

If someone is so starved for human companionship that she can talk through Beethoven's "Ninth Symphony," there's something wrong in her life. She paid money to listen to the musicians. She's sitting in an uncomfortable seat in a venue without enough ladies' bathrooms. It's a little too warm in here. Why would she choose this, of all places, to have a tête-à-tête with her neighbor? Starbucks is far more conducive to a cozy meeting among friends. Or the local swanky bar. Or a little restaurant. Or even her living room. Did it ever occur to her to invite the human being with whom she is in such rapt conversation to her home? Her companion would love to sit on her sofa and drink a cup of tea. But she's too reserved to say so. She's her symphony buddy, that lady whose husband also hates classical music, so they get season tickets together. But it never occurs to them to deepen the friendship, to take it home. Instead of having a coffee after the concert and discussing the way the music transported them, they catch up on the gossip throughout all the movements, not even pausing for the magnificent choral passages in the "Ode to Joy." I, on the other hand, am not sure whether my sobs are for the beauty of the music or the disappointment of the having the music spoiled for me by their conversation.

Musical events have been wrecked for me since the dot-com boom. Before that time, people sat quietly at the opera (or were asked to leave by the usher) or stood and danced to the rock band. Perhaps they'd call out requests or ask their neighbor to pass the joint, but, other than that, the music was audible. Wasn't it?

I'm especially disgusted with the chit chat that goes on at the ballet. In an era when more and more ballet companies are cutting their orchestras and moving to using recorded music to cut costs, we should be extremely grateful to companies that keep their orchestras. Pacific Northwest Ballet is such a company. They have a wonderful orchestra. Occasionally, they use recorded music for a specific dance, like William Forsythe's "One Flat Thing, Reproduced," which uses a musical composition by Thom Willems. I love that rep company and the recorded music is an amazing and integral part of it. And yet, I am glad not every dance comes with recorded music. Seattlites are so lucky to have live musicians in the orchestra pit. Doesn't the rest of the audience see that? How can they take such beauty for granted? Would they really buy season tickets to the ballet if there were no music? I go to the ballet for the dance, to be sure, but for me the whole experience of the dance is suspended in the music. It is the music that induces the rapid beating of my heart, the lump in my throat, the clenching of my muscles. It is the dance that stops my heart, slows my breathing, alters time and allows me to watch in a state of suspended animation. It is the music that afterward brings me back to life. The music is Frankenstein's spark, the thing that animates the livid flesh, the thing that sets to beating the stopped heart.

Seattle Opera, like Pacific Northwest Ballet, is one of the city's gems. While the ushers don't eject those who talk during the opera, they get one thing just right. The Seattle Opera starts on time. This is a courtesy to those who are punctual and a bane to those who are not. I am one who, while trying to be punctual, ends up being late. I learned early on to allow two hours to get to the opera on a Friday night, even though the same drive only takes ten minutes on a Sunday morning. Yes, that's how bad the traffic to Seattle Center (if you're not from Seattle, think Space Needle) is on a weekend night. It's wonderful to have the opera, the ballet, the theaters, the science museum and the Space Needle all in the same area. But it makes traffic and parking a nightmare. So, one night, I left perhaps fifteen minutes later than usual. I arrived at the parking lot, which did not have a Full sign out front. I drove all the way to the top level and all around the top level till I found the one spot that was left. This all took about fifteen minutes. The bottom line: by the time I reached McCaw Hall, all the bells had rung.

Now, if you miss the bells that signal the opera has started, you won't be seated till the next act. McCaw Hall has TV monitors is the lobbies on each floor, so that if you are late you can watch and listen. I tried each floor. Nowhere could I hear the opera. All the other latecomers, rather than watching the monitors, stood talking to their fellows. I was ready to scream. I mean, come on people, it's *Tosca*. Does the virtuosity of your scintillating conversation rival Puccini's genius for melody and harmony?

In a snit, I flounced up to the top floor, where my seat was. With nothing better to do, I decided to check my makeup in the ladies'. On the way, I passed the single-toilet family bathroom. Music was spilling from it. I entered and closed the door behind me. There in the ceiling was a speaker. While I had no idea what was happening on stage, I could at least *hear* the music. Which was better than I could say even for my regular seat in the hall. The bathroom was silent. No one was talking. I looked over at the lone toilet, locked the door, and settled in to the best seat in the house.

I wonder if there were speakers in the bathroom at the Oracle Arena, where I saw The Who?

I've seen The Who many times. The worst shows were right in the heart of Silicon Valley. Instead of hearing the music, all I could hear were the dot com yuppies in front of me bragging about how much they spent on their tickets and how many beers they had drunk. It must be nice to be able to afford to spend that kind of money for a show you aren't even going to listen to. For me, the price of each ticket came dearly. I treasured each ticket I scrimped and saved for. Each one was an opportunity—and that's how I saw it, an opportunity—to see one of the best rock and roll bands of all time.

There were plenty of other lousy audiences besides the ones in Mountain View.

"Smash your guitar, Pete!" the drunken idiot behind me yelled. "Smash your guitar!"

"You moron," I felt like saying. "Pete Townshend hasn't smashed a guitar in decades."

It was 2002. John Entwistle, The Who's bassist, had just died the day before their North American tour was set to begin. Pete seemed angry at such a loss, such a waste (Entwisle's death was attributed to a cocaine-induced heart attack.) We were at the Hollywood Bowl, the first show of the tour (after some schedule shuffling due to John's death). Of course Pete didn't smash his guitar. Not then. And I, who had been dead wrong about Pete not smashing his guitar in decades (he'd done it just seven months earlier in Portsmouth), felt smug.

At the Gorge in Washington state, we sat in the sun, waiting for The Who to play. It was July; the sun beats down late into the evening in Washington in the summer. The sun descended as the music ascended. The set list before encores was a mix of hits ending with "Won't Get Fooled Again." At the end of that song, Pete went into a long guitar solo. Then he took what looked like a spontaneous swipe at the microphone with the guitar, knocking the mic stand to the ground. It was thrilling. Before I knew what was happening, the guitar had swung up over his head and was arcing down into the amplifier, as if of its own volition. Again and again Pete smashed the guitar into the amp. Time took a funny sidestep to the right. My heart was beating fast or not beating at all. A little trickle of sweat on my upper lip joined the drenched rest of me. Was that me gasping? Bam. A discordant scream from the dying guitar.

In reviewing video of the event, I see less spontaneity, more intention to smash the guitar. There was never any question that the guitar, not the microphone stand, was Townshend's intended victim.

I can see why he was so angry. The loss of John was a great loss. In 2000, my brother and I traveled to Europe for my brother's thirty-fifth birthday. We saw The Who twice on that trip, once at Wembley Arena and once at the Royal Albert Hall. The Royal Albert Hall show short-circuited my brain. John Entwistle played bass like no one else. His fingers moved so fast you couldn't discern their individual movements. I'm not kidding; it was like a blur. I've never seen such talent so close.

Wembley was another great show. Except that because of me we were late. Because we were late, we missed the opening act. It proved to be Joe Strummer from The Clash. He died before we had another chance to see him.

But we did see The Who. And back then anyway, and there, the audience was silent except for their applause and shouts of approval between songs. It was how it should be. It was warm, friendly, connected. Without speaking, we were all one in that audience. The music united us. It wasn't our cell phones that tethered us to humanity—it was our respect for the music. That shared respect built an instant community. We were there, *together*, having the same experience, having maybe ten thousand different experiences at the same time. There was a unity that transcended all the loneliness of thousands of souls in that arena that night.

That unity carried over after the concert. We spilled out of the arena, smiling, laughing, talking to our neighbors. No one minded our American accents. Our English friends embraced us. No one pulled out his cell phone to start texting. We looked at each other, looked into each other's open eyes and saw living human beings looking back, saw what makes us more than human. My brother and I struck up a conversation with a couple of young men on the Tube (London's subway). I couldn't have agreed with my new companion more when he said:

"It was a privilege to see them, mate. A real privilege."

$\vdots$

22

$\vdots$

Songs about Angels

Judith Carroll

Once inside your head, they snowball.

Pretty Little Angel Eyes with its *oo-oo*s
and choreographed dance steps
morphs into Earth Angel, and you're barely
past *Will you be mine*, before you're humming
Teen Angel, a song you loathed even in 1960
when girls you knew spent hours at the jukebox,
hankies wadded in their fists.

You much preferred Angel Baby, *my angel baby*,
with Rosie's high voice and the sultry sax
bringing the gym lights down to dim,
Kenny Johnson's breath on the top of your head,
your body tossing coins between Devil or Angel.

$\vdots$

24

$\vdots$

Follow the Music

Patti Cavaliere

At the entrance of Seaside Park, I buy my wristband for the annual Gathering of the Vibes festival and wander into the crowd. An invisible mist distills the ocean air with cultural blends of Mexican, Thai and plumes of marijuana. Every inch of lawn is covered with a tent, a blanket, a body, like pixels washed ashore by the sea. But the park weathered a turbulent storm since the event here last summer. So had I.

I've twisted white-and-purple feather boas across the back of my chair so it will be easy to spot because last year Brian and I had become disoriented trying to find our way back to our chairs. Little did I know then that Brian would spend his last days on earth in that same state of mind, frustrated, unable to form words, unable finally, to remember me as the wife who had shared dinners with him and danced to music. After losing him to cancer, I began to compartmentalize my life—days before Brian, days after.

The sun is starting to set—tie-dyed colors filling the horizon. I pass the Karma Wash, an arched tunnel decorated with flowers, streamers and a strobe light. A man, blond, with glasses, smiles at me like he recognizes me, his eyes sad and reaching. I return a timid smile and turn away, then prop open my canvas chair. Once it gets dark, there will be little chance of finding a familiar face.

The full moon rises into a nebulous shadow streaking the heavens. I sip smooth rustic java, let it settle into my taste buds like fine chocolate.

On the Green Vibes stage, the band is playing, master puppeteers working the crowd like guitar strings to the pluck of their picks. Moonlight floods the sky with soft gray glows of a campsite lantern and beneath it, I am one of 25,000. The tune plays me like a skeleton key rattling inside a keyhole, trying to find the way to open me up again. It seeps into my soul like the Holy Spirit at a southern revival, but my spirit is blocked.

Across the field a tree flickers, enveloped in magical green laser lights. There's so much to see in the dark. Like my summers growing up in Bridgeport, when my mother brought my sister here and me, set a blanket on the lawn beneath a large Maple like that one. Then we'd hop barefoot across the asphalt to the beach. I remember low tide with fondness for its kindness to my tender feet, the long stretch of cool sucking sand, rippled with the imprint of waves and smooth iridescent seashells. The rhythm of the sea crashes over me like it was yesterday.

I see another memory as the dark air fills with lively chords – I am thirteen-years-old in my parent's basement. It's cold and damp and my fingers are too short to bend around the neck of the white solid-body guitar my father bought me for my birthday.

Then he and my mom separated, he joined a band, and met a woman one night while playing at a wedding. For years I blamed the guitar.

A fine rain starts. While sipping my coffee, the rain drips off the spokes of the umbrella and the blond man appears beside me, turns his palm up and holds out a lit joint.

"No. Thanks." I lift my umbrella, which he takes as an invitation to step into my personal space.

"You were smart to bring an umbrella," he says, grabbing the handle. His cool skin touches mine and my hand flinches. He takes a drag and my lungs lunge toward the skunky pungent odor. "Are you sure?" he asks, again offering me the joint.

My shoulder lifts. "Okay. Maybe a little."

Within minutes, my head swells like one of the balloons floating into the clouds; I feel my eyes pinch back into slits.

"I noticed you when you first walked by," he says. "You look like the actress in *Dr. Zhivago*."

"Julie Christie?" The image I remember: high cheek bones, a serious mouth, her blonde bang swept across her forehead. The atmosphere mellows. "No one's told me before."

"You smiled at me when you passed by," he says.

Had I smiled on some subconscious level when I passed him earlier? His face is subtle, delicate nose, expressive brows.

"I was looking for friends. I circled the Artisan Village, the not-for-profit booths." I offer him a sip of coffee, not expecting him to take it.

"My name is Jeff."

I feel the cold rain drizzling on my shoulders.

On stage the band winds riffs like a mystical cyclone. People start twirling, leaping like spiders. Was it weed or mushrooms, or joy?

I'm bashful when I try to dance until I see Jeff, his long torso bent at the waist, hopping leg to leg and shaking his head. Music consumes the air and I want so much for it to consume me, too.

"Come meet my friend," he says when the rain stops.

I scoot between the one-foot line of lawn chairs and shake his friend's hand, bopping as we are introduced. It's difficult to converse over the volume, and a relief not to have to. Instead, we exchange smiles and our hands brush each other.

I lose track of time.

Before the music stops, Jeff puts his hand on my shoulder to get my attention.

"I need to leave. I'm not driving and my friend wants to go. He lives out of state. I'd like to see you again."

He hands me a pen and the envelope from his tickets. I write my name and number. We hug good-bye.

⁓ ⁓ ⁓

The next time I hear from Jeff, we make plans to meet for a September dinner when the moon is full again. Could I pick him up at the train station? He'll take the train in from New York City.

I'm waiting in my car, parked in front of Union Station. Jeff locates my car and gets into the passenger seat; he's wearing a dress shirt and pants and carrying a black leather briefcase. He leans over to kiss my cheek. I have not seen him in four weeks and I've never seen him in daylight. His hair is the color of snow, not blond, and his skin is the color of eggshell with a shadow of silver beard that has a translucent appearance. I think of the Julie Christie comment. It should have tipped me off to his age—*Dr. Zhivago* was released four years before the Woodstock festival of '69.

"You're a good dancer," he says. "I noticed that about you." The more he talks, the more I like him.

"You made the night fun for me, too, Jeff. I hadn't danced—in a while."

We drive to the Italian restaurant where he made reservations. Soon after we arrive and place our order, it begins to pour. We toast the rumble of thunder, the lightening electrifying the sky, the night like this when we met under my umbrella. But was this bad karma or my own foolishness? Had the intoxication of that night rendered me blind to notice what I do now—an expensive gold wedding band around his ring finger.

"You're married, Jeff?"

He places his elbows on the table and covers his fingers with his right hand. He nods as the waitress places the salad before us, sweet Tuscan peppers, tangy balsamic vinegar. A metallic flavor turns in my mouth before I begin to eat. I think of my smooth white guitar, my parent's divorce. History repeating itself.

"I don't date married men." I lower my gaze into my salad and slide some of it onto my fork.

"Will you keep an open mind?"

Open mind? What does that mean? My mind flits off into tangents—was he leaving his wife?

"Let's order the mussels gorgonzola and share," Jeff says.

My eyes snap up to meet his. Mussels gorgonzola. *Brian had loved them.*

When our meals come, he asks if I'd like a taste of his swordfish. I give him a portion of my steak pizzaiola and roasted potatoes.

"So what concert should we go to next?"

"We can't go together, Jeff." *But I would like to.* "Are you separated?"

"No. The marriage is good." His voice deepens when he says this. "Except, my wife doesn't enjoy music at all. It doesn't move in her the way it moves me and you."

Me and you. The words feel too intimate, they link our lives. "I can't see you again, Jeff."

"You said you'd been married. Can't you relate? Music is too much a part of me to live my life without it." His brow shortens with wrinkles; his smart eyes seem to search for my answer.

Was this all that we have together—a love of music, the one thing missing in his marriage?

"I feel good being around you. I can be myself," he says.

At one of the Artesian tents at The Vibes concert a young woman had stood beside me with naked peach-size breasts painted like flower blossoms. She leaned over the table of silver jewelry, rows of crafted leathers, blown glass items, mostly pipes. She was fairy-like, long straight blonde hair, barefoot and carefree. Was I ever so carefree, before life had handed me a dead husband, and now a married man who wants me to share a secret part of his life?

"Let's follow the music," he says, playful and tender.

Follow the music. No sticky sex, no waiting up for long distance phone calls when he travels, no holiday dinners with my family expecting to meet him. It sounds easy enough.

The next day I want to call him to thank him for dinner, but as I open my phone and stare at his number, my phone rings. It's Jeff. "Other worldly," he says when I tell him I was just thinking of him.

We meet at an outdoor music festival on a seaside shore of a town not far from where this all started. It's a halfway point between our homes, and our very separate lives. The October moon is full.

Jeff holds me tight when we hug.

It's okay. We're only following the music.

He has been traveling for work, a production company for theater and arts. From his briefcase he digs out a small wrapped box with a lime green bow and funky scrolled paper. When I unwrap the package the name on the box says *Moonstruck, Hand Crafted Artisan Chocolates.* There is a silhouette of a crescent moon with a naked piper dancing inside the crescent. I open the box of chocolate truffles and read the hand-written note that Jeff tucked inside the tissue paper. *Once you realize we are connected, we will be fine.*

We share truffles decorated like costume jewelry. Their scent lights up my olfactory bulb. Until now, I never realized how much chocolate smells like vanilla.

I imagine it looks like we're lovers, rather than music lovers.

I wouldn't be here with him otherwise, but when he takes my hand and we walk toward the stage I begin to doubt myself. As the band plays we occasionally exchange sidelong glances where our eyes connect, but mostly it's me, or him, looking over our shoulders to watch each other dance. *This is the only gift he wants from me.*

When I see how much Jeff feels the song, I close my eyes and lift my arms away from my waist, untwist my hips, set myself free.

After the band finishes we walk across the town green to a Victorian restaurant for a late night dinner.

"I know this is hard for you, that we can't spend more time together. You can ask me anything," he says.

Because he says this, it makes me less curious about his life. And the time lapse between our visits creates a barrier for my emotion. It can only be about the music that we are connected.

As we sit on the wrap around porch beside the spindle railing and look up to find the moon, it starts to rain.

The full moon has come and gone since that August night I'd met Jeff at The Vibes concert, but we talk every few weeks on the phone about his foreign wife, my recent job change, his six-year-old son.

I take the train into the city; I'm standing in the cold outside the B.B. King venue for the concert that we bought tickets to see. My phone rings.

"I'm not going to make it to the concert. I'm so sorry." Jeff's eighty-hour work week, frequent travel, the demands of being a thoughtful father and devoted son to his elderly mother, have thinned his resistance. His voice sounds as if he has rusted vocal chords. He's almost home now, his cell phone is fading, "I'll miss you," he says before he has to go.

Disappointment sifts through me like a cloud, but it's hard to tell Jeff I'll miss him.

On my drive home I listen to a CD that Brian once loved because it makes me feel like Brian's still with me. All the rain inside me has stopped now. I can follow the music alone.

Maybe It Happened This Way

Susan Chiavelli

You can be anyone you want in this story. There's a girl. There's a boy. There's a party. You can be her, or you can be him. You can even be them. If you need to know what they look like, just dig out your high-school yearbook. God. Those hairstyles! Those clothes!

The girl walks out the front door to meet her boyfriend. Her mother and father sit in the living room listening to the radio. Bye, they say, to their invisible daughter. Have a nice time.

The door closes behind her, and she skips down the porch steps; her heels tap out promising music in the still night—a song of expectation. She's bathed in moonlight and filled with yearning. By the time she reaches the bottom of the stairs, she's stepped into another world. What will she be? Something's waiting to happen. She feels it buzzing all around her. There's music playing in her head, but she doesn't know the words. She hears his car two blocks away, and the rumble of it stirs her. In the dark shelter of the newly budded dogwood tree she rolls up her waistband so her skirt exposes her thighs. She steps out from the darkness, looks down and is pleased at her long-drink-of-water legs gilded with moonlight, like the glossy magazine girls'. You know; those silent, smiling, one-dimensional girls with nothing to say. Still, she longs to look like them.

The boy drives up in his car. He has all that power under his hood. She smiles. The type of car doesn't really matter. You pick the make and year; I'll pick the color. It's baby blue and gleaming under the street lamp. He polished it all day, and while he rubbed and rubbed, he thought about the girl – her legs, her tits, her eyes. The muscles in his right hand ache from all that rubbing. He opens the car door, and she slides across the seat next to him in one graceful move, natural, not practiced. His hand falls to her bare thigh, and the ache intensifies as he kisses her lightly on the lips. There's a love song playing on the radio. She thinks maybe it will be their song. He's been waiting for this all day.

The girl thinks maybe she loves him. Maybe that's who she'll be? A girl in love? She looks in the rearview mirror and moistens her lips.

They drive to the party. He turns off the highway onto a dirt road, and the headlights illuminate the No Trespassing sign. It's buried behind Queen Anne's lace and splattered with bullet holes. The girl looks at the ragged holes and knows how they got there. She sees pictures in her mind as clearly as a movie: Boys laughing and whooping it up. Harmless target practice—boys with their need to puncture. It's a warning in the moonlight, stay away from here, stay away. But they don't. They drive deeper into the woods. Gnarled trees. No turning back.

They pull up to an abandoned house. You know what it looks like. Don't pretend you don't; you've been there. If there's one to be found, boys will find it. Flickering light from a kerosene lamp licks at the front window; giant shadows splash against a backdrop of jagged trees. Music drifts outside. You pick the song. There's always one or two that linger from the old days.

The boy and girl hold hands and go inside. Don't they make a sweet couple?

There's a keg in the corner and a beat-up wooden stool by the window. Kids are milling around, drinking. The boy gets some beer and goes to find his friends. Guys cluster in the back of the room by what looks like a partial lean-to wall. Something's going on behind the shadows. The girl knows this because there's nervous laughter, and people keep glancing over their shoulders toward the back of the room. From where she's standing she can't see anything, but she feels it—a deep black pit to slide into.

She looks around. Her girlfriends are in their usual circle in the remnants of a kitchen. She joins them. They give her some sloe gin in a paper cup. They're already tipsy and giggling. You know these girls. They're on the junior prom committee, and it's their job to turn the gym into Paris. The girl is on the committee with them because she knows lots of songs in old movies. She's the one who came up with the theme: "Three Coins in a Fountain." It didn't matter to anyone that the song's about a fountain in Rome. Besides, the girl plans to go to Paris someday. And she will, in April.

She takes a long hard drink in order to catch up. Her girlfriends seem to know what's going on behind the lean-to wall and whisper about it. The girl knows it's that. She doesn't know how she knows these things, but she does. She sometimes hears people say things they swear they never said out loud, and they look at her with fear and glance away. Her grandmother says it's a *gift*. But she's not sure she wants it.

There's more commotion from the back now. Some of the boys have pushed a bench over to the lean-to wall and they're standing on it and peering over the top and cheering and laughing. What? The girl says. What? Don't go back there, the prom committee says. It's just her, that girl. You choose her name. Every school has one.

The prom committee closes the circle. They have dresses to discuss. Snow-white satin, with straps or without? No, without is too risqué. Cotton-candy pink chiffon, and buttercup-yellow voile, and spring-green brocade. Virgin-green, she thinks, but she doesn't say it. She listens to the girl-talk and imagines her friends in these dresses gathered together in a pastel bouquet, which is how they'll close ranks against her when they see the dress she copied from *Glamour*: royal-blue satin with a sequin bodice. There's a problem she doesn't mention. The sweetheart neckline is too plunging—more revealing on her body than on the wispy flat-chested girl drawn on the front of the pattern envelope. What a surprise when she tried it on—all that cleavage! All her babysitting money spent on those shimmering neon breasts. The girls won't like it, but the boys will. You don't need a gift to know that.

She finishes another drink and bravery surges through her. She tells the prom committee she wants to find her boyfriend. They buy it; after all, that's what they all want.

She works her way through the milling crowd toward the ruckus in the back. Somehow she knows he's there. There's a glimpse through the open doorway of the lean-to room: An old mattress on the floor. Isn't there always one of those in a place like this? From where she stands she can smell the mixture of spilled beer and mildew. Her eyes adjust to the darkness. There must be a little window in the back, because now she sees it, a bare white leg frozen in a slanted shaft of moonlight, an unmoving leg like a store mannequin's lying against the stained ticking of the mattress. And then one of the boys fills up the doorway as he leaves the room; he staggers against the doorjamb and fumbles to zip up his pants. Their eyes meet and he's not ashamed. Too drunk for that. Another boy goes in to take his turn. The girl quickly sees that there's a line. Some of the boys are still standing on the bench and hanging over the wall, watching and jeering. One of them has a flashlight and he's pointing it into the darkness beyond the wall, and the girl knows what it's illuminating. The boys' eyes are gleaming in the lantern light, and the one with the flashlight turns to smile at her like a naughty boy with a secret in second grade. She doesn't smile back. The music keeps playing on the radio.

Her boyfriend is standing next to her now. Come on, he says. Let's get out of here. He takes her arm to lead her away but she says no, and she pushes his hand off. Make them stop. He shrugs and says he didn't do anything. Come on, don't be mad. She says, tell them it's not right. That girl is drunk. Passed out. She doesn't even know what's happening! He says let's go. No! She screams it this time, and it surprises everyone, including herself. People turn to look. He's tugging at her arm now, and she pushes him away. The boys standing on the bench glance down at her from above and laugh. Their faces remind her of leering jack-o-lanterns. The one with the flashlight shines it in her eyes, blinding her; her boyfriend grabs her arm and drags her away. There's no release from him this time. He's stronger. It all comes down to that. She yells again and looks to her friends for help, but the prom committee looks away. They pretend to see nothing.

She's outside now on the sloping front porch where the world is strangely tilted, alone with her boyfriend. She's embarrassed to be crying. It's stupid; she doesn't even know that girl. He kisses her, and she lets him. She could have been that girl. He slides his hand underneath her blouse, and then underneath her hiked-up skirt. She lets him do that, too. Everything is happening, and this can't be undone.

At school on Monday she'll be standing with the prom committee as they whisper about that girl, what happened at the party. She'll remain silent, trying to remember if maybe she's that girl? But that girl won't have a date for the prom. They'll watch her walk alone in the halls with her head hanging. See, they'll whisper. See. The boy who had the flashlight will whistle long train whistles whenever he sees that girl, and the prom committee won't get it.

One day before the prom, the girl will find herself alone with that girl in the lavatory in front of the mirror, each watching their own reflection side-by-side as they slide lipstick on. She'll want that mouth in the mirror to speak, but it won't belong to her. It will look silent and glossy like the pretty girls' mouths in magazines. Besides, there are no words to undo what's been done.

The girl will be quiet at home and no one will notice. She'll not find any joy in the prom committee. She'll see how futile it is to try to make what happened into Paris. Paris! But she'll help decorate the gym with crepe paper anyway. When no one's looking she'll throw a coin in the cardboard fountain, her dreams unaltered. Fragments of the song haunt her: "Which one will the fountain choose?"

Or maybe it happened this way... A girl and a boy went to a party in an abandoned house in the woods. Her friends gave her a drink of sloe gin and it made her foolish. She had another and another. She remembers the yeasty smell of spilled beer and mildew, the flickering lantern light, the hideous jack-o-lantern faces with gleaming eyes hanging above her in the dark, the shaft of moonlight penetrating the broken window. The relentless music. But she remembers nothing else. Nothing except the blood on her dress and the blood on her white underwear and the searing burning pain that is her only companion for days afterward. There is one girl at school who looks at her with pity in the mirror in the girl's room, and she hates her the most.

Or maybe it happened this way... A girl and a boy went to a party at an abandoned house in the woods. Her friends gave her a drink of sloe gin and it made her brave and foolish all at once. She had another.

There's a commotion in the back. She works her way through the milling crowd and gets a glimpse through the open doorway of a lean-to room. There's a smelly mattress on the floor. Dirty, stained. Now she sees it, a bare white leg frozen in moonlight, an unmoving leg like a store mannequin's. And then a boy staggers against the doorjamb and fumbles to zip up his pants. Their eyes meet and he's not ashamed. There's a line. The boys on the bench are still hanging over the wall, watching. One of them has a flashlight and he's pointing it downward and the girl knows what it's illuminating. She's amazed at their lack of shame and then at her own for watching them watch. Their eyes are gleaming in the lantern light, and one of them, the one with the flashlight smiles at her. She doesn't smile back.

Her boyfriend is standing next to her now. Come on, he says. Let's go. He tries to lead her away, but she says, no, and pushes his hand off. Make them stop. He shrugs. Come on, don't be mad, he says. I didn't go in there. I didn't even watch. It's not right, she says. That girl's passed out. He says, let's go. No! She screams it this time and flings his hand away. His mouth falls slackly open; he's wary of her resolve. The boy with the flashlight turns and shines it down in her eyes, and all the boys laugh at what they see there. This is the moment. It all comes down to this. She kicks hard at the bench, and it tips out from underneath the boys and they tumble to the floor in a drunken slobbering heap. Everyone at the party stops to watch, their eyes looking at a girl they don't know. Who is that girl? Who is she? Her boyfriend moves toward her, but she picks up the wooden stool with peeling paint and holds it high above her head. He stops. All the boys stop. Even the boy in the lean-to room stops. Time stops. She smashes the stool through the window, and it shatters everything with a satisfying crash—past, present, future—slivers of glass burst into the night like wishing stars falling from the sky; they hang suspended for a moment, and after this nothing will ever be the same...except for her dream of Paris.

Years later the girl will go to Paris and learn it rains there in April, but she won't really be surprised. She knows by now that life is not a song. She'll have a son and a daughter of her own, and she'll watch them grow. The time will come when they'll walk out the door and down the steps to a party. She'll see their dreams glistening in the moonlight, and she'll remember the music that has no words. She'll call out to them. Wait, don't go. Not yet. Did I ever tell you a story? About a party in an abandoned house in the woods? There's a girl. There's a boy. And you can be anyone in this story.

36

October Dirge

Jan Chronister

Thirty-degree sky
clear at seven
fills up with dustballs of gray
erasing hopes of hanging out sheets.

In the silence between cycles
I say goodbye to the garden.

The dog runs in and out
stenciling mud on rugs.
I stack wood
laying dry oak bones
to form a closely fitted keyboard.
Each one sounds its own tone—
a song of summer I forgot.

Flute

Terry Cox-Joseph

Low moan of Cherokee flute
plump with sound
gentle with promise
flowing with peace
play for me.
And play again.

Is there a god to whom we kneel
or is this song a gift to our souls,
encircling rustling leaves with tendrils
that resonate within the long wooden reed
until it becomes its own god?

Sufi Music

Daphne Crocker-White

A tree teases me
with too many shadows
the color of clouds
people have white lights
around their heads
a bud as large as a fist
suckles its petals.
I worry it will be forced
into a vase
I spin and spin
in my white dress
see only belts....see only nothing
I am an orbit....a star
spiral between wind and fire
double back to earth and water
Cannot... will not stop
if there even was a before
I cannot remember

In the morning the bud breaks open trumpets yellow with blood red
        streaks

40

One Note, Softly

Lee Cunningham

Dolores Thompson sat and pondered the case file in her hands. She was alone at 7:00 in the evening on a week night, just sitting in the hand-me-down 1958 Ford from her dad. She had no desire to go into her tiny, rented house; instead, she sat alone, reading, turning pages and occasionally, weeping.

The day had been special. With no prior indication, the powers-that-be had assigned her to work with a patient who had been in that Central Wisconsin VA hospital for over twenty years since the end of World War II. She was reviewing his medical records.

She had trained as a nurse with psychology as a major field, and worked almost exclusively with male patients and the occasional wounded female jeep driver—all casualties exposed to the trauma of war. Dolly worked with men damaged in battle, mainly from the European Theatre where they'd faced the Axis forces of Mussolini and Hitler. All these men were at least twenty years older than the day they'd enlisted—the day after the Japanese had bombed Pearl Harbor on Sunday, December 7, 1941.

On her off-time, Dolly tried not to think of bombs, grenades, and battlefield explosions; instead, she played the piano and organ in the church and directed the choir made up of Norwegians who loved to sing and enjoyed full-bodied voices.

Dolly's head jerked up suddenly as if she were searching for a light switch. She had been so engrossed in her reading, she hadn't realized daylight had faded into near-darkness.

She had been reviewing the chart of the patient she had been requesting to work with for several months. No, she was wrong; it had actually been years. Dolly had spotted Ray early on, but had not asked about him until she'd settled into her surroundings and the routine of being a specialized nursing staff of one.

Seeing Ray had reminded her of her friend Rebecca, the nurse she had shadowed in actual practice. Rebecca had a patient with a similar history and complaints. That patient had been sitting for years, thought to be deaf and without speech. He never made any noises from his throat, and displayed no efforts to communicate, not even with hand motions or drawings.

Dolly remembered that Rebecca knew of a large storage space for donated musical instruments. One day, Rebecca had taken this patient there and sat down with him in the midst of these instruments used for special events. He seemed most relaxed around percussion instruments—drums, bells, blocks, chimes, a piano, and a tiny triangle with its striker tied to it.

She had shaken, struck or rattled everything nearby to let him hear what they sounded like. Dolly had watched all this intently, noting the man had perked up a little. When Rebecca was busy looking for other instruments, he had carefully picked up a small hammer attached to a metal triangle. He considered it for a moment and then delicately touched the little hammer to the triangle and listened, seeming pleased with himself as a smile briefly softened his face. Rebecca had swerved around and shot Dolly such a look.

"That wasn't me. That was him."

Rebecca whispered, "Are you sure?"

Dolly, finally realizing what had just happened, nodded with a smile. The man had stepped out from his closed-up self for a moment.

"Progress is being made," Rebecca had murmured as she patted his shoulder and allowed herself a huge, face-splitting grin.

Dolly had left her work with Rebecca shortly after that, and gone to work for the VA, but she never forgot the man. Now she needed to know what had become of this patient.

Darkness had set in. Dolly gathered all her papers and walked briskly toward the dark house. She had been focused so intently on this new case, she couldn't remember where her phone numbers were. It was already 9:00; time was getting short. Rebecca might have early starts in the mornings. Hopefully, she dialed the home number for her old friend.

"Hello?"

"Rebecca? This is Dolly. Dolly Thompson. Remember me?" She said in a voice pitched high with anxiety.

"Oh, for heaven's sake. How are you? Are you still at the VA? It's been a while, hasn't it? Time flies."

42

"How I'd love to catch up, but I've a new case and need to know how things worked out with the patient who reacted to that instrument—the triangle. Did he ...?

"That was a real magic moment for you, wasn't it? What do you want to know? He advanced somewhat and impressed his family so much they took him home!" She paused, excited. "Tell me about crazy. They were so excited. Sort of like they probably were when he'd said his first word ...like "Mama" or some swear word he'd heard when his Dad had hit his own thumb with a hammer." She laughed. "How's tricks there?"

They talked until Dolly could believe she was on a right track and promised to call back on the weekend. Rebecca said she'd do some follow-up on the "triangle" patient as soon as she could remember his name.

If only they could find a "key" to reach some of these patients, but who would bet on that? Dolly had been looking forward to studying new techniques in communications therapy in the summer, which could help, but would also interrupt her work with Ray for six weeks, and that kind of change in his routines could mean losing any gains he might make, however tiny.

Ray's records included his family's descriptions of his former self, which said he'd liked music, dancing and singing. So Dolly took him to the social room and sat down at the piano with him. She played some jitterbug pieces on the piano. No reaction at all.

I'll keep trying, she told herself. Something has to snap him out of this place he's in.

A few days later, Dolly came home for work crying deep, heavy sobs from another day of failure. She called Rebecca to say there was no change, none whatsoever, in Ray's condition. Rebecca wished her well, encouraging her to be patient, and then she sighed.

Another time, several days later, Dolly slammed out some boogie-woogie, sliding up and down the keyboard and thumping out the beat as he sat next to her on the piano bench. Had she seen his index finger move just a bit, keeping time with the music?

So the next day she tried it again. She sat him to her right and did a medley from the 1940s: jitterbug, swing, and popular songs like "Boogie-Woogie Bugle Boy." She let herself move to the upbeat rhythms with a freedom she'd never before felt, and raised her hands high above the keyboard and dropped them down hard in exaggerated goofiness thinking he might laugh, but he didn't. That night, she spoke with Rebecca again, trying to maintain hope.

This went on for several weeks. "Summer school" was coming up soon, so Dolly packed her things, getting ready to go home to her parents' house and then on to her classes.

The next day she led Ray to the piano and played him some piano classics from one of his own lesson books his sister had brought for Dolly—simplified pieces for beginning students. When she finished, she rested her arms and hands in her lap. Joe sat motionless, saying nothing as Dolly regarded the trees and flowers outside. As she looked out across the gardens, her eye caught some tiny movement to her right.

He lifted his hand and extended his index finger to point to the keyboard. It landed on Middle C and pushed the key down quietly. A soft note sounded in the stillness. When Dolly saw his eyes brighten with pride, she felt in herself a swelling emotion new to her.

She looked at him sideways and whispered with an intensity from deep within, "Progress is being made!"

44

Rusty Heart

Marcy Darin

Steel on steel
winding twenty miles through
forests of ancient water towers and lots filled with broken glass
as if a pinata were pierced and bitterness sprinkled
on streets named for dead presidents.
Rails on stilts
forged a century ago by hungry men who built
Nelson Algren's "dark girders of the city's rusty heart"
their thrumming
like water running over dinner dishes in a kitchen sink
lulling an anxious child to sleep.
Wheels clacking like an old fashioned pull toy on wood floors
through West Side streets laid out on graph paper
past schools with concrete playgrounds
intersecting dreams deferred.

Leonard Bernstein Speaks to Me

Carol V. Davis

10 pm. I drag myself to the car.
Even the security booth is abandoned.
I slide in, check the backseat, lock the doors.
So dark I cannot fit the key into its hole.
The engine grumbles,
roused unhappily from its slumber.
On the radio a man lectures on the symphony.
It is Lennie, a voice I have known since childhood.

Lennie, tell me more, that everything will turn around.
Money appear in my bank account, a discovered concerto.
Creditors dropped like a revised score.
The largo waiting to catch me before I fall.
Let me understand how the world is larger than a symphony,
such intricate parts, the delight of a piccolo,
the torrent of a kettle drum.
Let me follow your baton as you gather up the violins,
whip them into a crescendo, rein them in,
calm them, then fool them into submission.

In a German Forest

Lois Edstrom

Lately I am drawn to the silhouette of treetops
in evening light, how a breeze stirs the leaves

exposing a silver underside and the trees sway
not exactly in rhythm, more a bending to the same impulse,

a slow tempo backlit by the moon,
seduction and fluidity of night.

Near Mittenwald trees make music.
Buyers tap trunks to hear

the soul of a violin longing to sing,
or a Bosendorfer's sonorous, complex heart.

I hear the haunting movement
of Beethoven's "Pathetique"

pulse within the fibers and juice
of evergreen, course through branches

to the uplifted tips of its needles,
compressed into rings and rings of years.

Birdsong

Donna L. Emerson

She spent two days with birds before her last surgery.
She walked the levees in Consumnes,
Talked to the white fronts, kingfishers, cinnamon teals.

Listened for the snow geese: was it too late?
Had they already scattered?
Searched off the main roads, back in the farmers'

ponds, wanting their chattering, their fly-ups,
a curtain of opals to sweep her clean
with wing flutter, see them swoop down

each one finding a perfect spot among
the others, without a squawk. To rest.

Flocks learn fifty calls from their parents, she tells me.
When they fly, they listen to other neighborhoods
of birds to see if they belong.

The closer the male and female are
in color, the more likely they'll mate for life.
Otherwise it's just for the season.

The only birds who can smell are the buzzards.
She admires their work. They are the nurses.

She told me she didn't think she'll die in surgery, later
this week, but if she does, she's filled herself with birdsong,
skeins of snow geese flying at dusk.

Listening to Brahms

Charles Fishman

A forest is laid waste. Birds sing
to each other, shaming the violins.
Rain drifts down in shadow torn
from the farthest sky.

Listening to Brahms, the oceans
prepare to die and black tsunamis hurry
toward the land. Cities darken, the membrane
over the earth's core parts.

We are listening to Brahms: the nineteenth century
taunts us. In the Sahel, the dead pile up. Sand gushes
like oil from the mouths of the Sahara. On Sinai, Silence
speaks in shrouds.

Rain falls with the ghost-arms of the forgotten. The orchestra
of birds plays on. Listening to Brahms, the percussionist
awaits his moment. It is Brahms who shatters the bow, who makes
the severed strings of the closing millennium   vibrate.

50

Cherry

Catherine Underhill Fitzpatrick

I learned how to braid an eight-strand lanyard at Camp Coureur des Bois. I learned how to fit the knock of an arrow into a bowstring, teepee my kindling, Allemande Left on a square dance floor, and fold an American flag into a perfect triangle, skills I regarded as critical in the summer of 1955 and have not required since.

It was a camper, a wiry hellion of a girl, who taught me the most durable lesson of all, a lesson set to campfire music.

Arrivals Day dawned as sultry as any other St. Louis summer morning, which is to say that by sunup the air was soup. After breakfast, my mother poured sweet tea into a thermos, wrapped two bologna sandwiches in waxed paper, and put the sack on the front seat her car. The morning dragged on; time is elastic when you're eight, going on nine. After an eternity of a few minutes duration, it was finally, finally, time to leave.

Nestled in the undulating foothills of the Ozarks, Camp Coureur des Bois sprawled across fifty acres of wildflower meadows, lazy creeks, and hardwood groves threaded with horse trails. The land had been wild for ages, rural for generations, and a camp for decades.

I shot out of the car and ran to the quadrangle. Scores of new campers were milling around a totem pole, waiting for something to happen. Mr. Franklin, the camp director, parted the crowd and strode officiously to the center. He was a squat, balding man, and when he raised a whistle and blew, the sound was shrill enough to file diamonds. After the girls in back stopped whispering, Mr. Franklin launched into an oration about Osage totems, Chickasaw customs, and French woodsmen, called coureur des bois. Twenty sweltering minutes later, he invited the parents to leave. Three girls promptly broke down in tears. One child dashed to her father's car, climbed in, and locked the doors. To staunch the flow of defectors, counselors struck up a rousing rendition of "This Land is Your Land." I turned in time to see Mom's DeSoto ease down the gravel drive, trailing twin contrails of dust.

Someone was calling my name, a counselor. I thought Miss Tina was prettier than Princess on "Father Knows Best," prettier even than the middle Lennon Sister. On the way to the cabins, I tried to stay close to the front of the line so I could watch her golden pony tail swing like a pendulum.

"Grace," Miss Tina said over her shoulder, "you're in Oak Leaf Cabin with Vickie, Mary Kay, and Cherry."

Cherry? That's a Jell-O flavor. I cracked a smile.

Cherry planted herself in front of me.

"One thing y'all needs keep in mind, new girl," she said. "My name ain't funny." Then she twanged my forehead so hard I stumbled backward.

Cherry looked to be about my age. She was taller by several inches, but skinny as a starveling. Her skin was so black her mosquito bite scratches looked like lines on a chalk board. Her blouse was faded, and her shoes were the kind of black high-top Keds boys wore; the laces limp and trailing.

Miss Tina was well ahead, chattering away. "We're the Muskrat Unit," she was saying. "Isn't that great? Muskrats are the best..."

Be glad we're not in Fox Unit," Vickie whispered. "Miss Jean makes Fox Unit go on nature walks to gather trash. Miss Tina's great. She gives out lemon drops and brown licorice swizzles at snack time, and during rest time she does our hair in French twists, if it's long enough."

Neither for the first time in my life nor the last, I cursed my short hair.

Oak Leaf Cabin was identical to all the others, which is to say it was closet-sized, dun-gray, and bestowed with the name of a tree.

"Pretty dinky," I said under my breath. Vickie snorted.

Two bunk beds, four shallow shelves, and four campers filled Oak Leaf cabin to capacity. Moving around required a sideways twist and precision footwork.

Vickie and Mary Kay had been cabin mates the previous year, and right off they snagged the bunk bed on the left. Cherry was ensconced in the lower bunk on the right. With a sigh, I tossed my bedroll to the top bunk and planted a foot on the metal frame, careful to avoid Cherry, her blanket, her pillow, her anything.

Quick as a striking copperhead, Cherry kicked my foot away. I tumbled backward and landed hard, rump-to-the-floor.

"What'd you do that for?" I said, willing myself to not cry.

"Top bed's mine. Been mine all summer. You on the bottom."

"But your stuff is—"

"Get your shit off that top bunk!"

I jumped up and grabbed my bedroll. Cherry leaped up, too, and stood behind me. I felt her breath on the back of my neck. Vickie devoted herself to organizing her toiletries on one of the shelves. Mary Kay demonstrated an extraordinary interest in pillow fluffing.

"Stop!" Cherry shouted. "Bottom bed's mine. Been mine all summer. You up there, girl."

I picked up my bedroll again, hoisted it to the top bunk, and clambered up. The mattress smelled like old pee. I wanted to go home.

Later, Vickie gave me the lowdown about Cherry.

"A church group in St. Louis pays the money for her to spend all summer here," Vickie said. "They probably figure camp will make Cherry turn out okay, but it isn't working. Last summer she stuffed a whole pancake in her mouth and spat it out, right onto the table. She even bragged about how she was gonna set Mr. Franklin's beagle on fire!"

Miss Tina blew her whistle. It was time for our camp tour. Vickie and I joined the other Muskrats on the path in front of the cabins.

"Over there, that's the mess hall," Miss Tina said, pointing to a log building with a deep front porch. "Our cooks specialize in hamburgers, sloppy joes, chili, and meat loaf ... anything with ground beef. And they never run out of bug juice."

I pinched my nose. "Bug juice! Yuck!"

Miss Tina laughed. "Bug juice is camp-talk for Kool-Aid."

Beyond the quadrangle, a large open-sided lodge commanded the top of a grassy rise.

"Each night after supper, the whole camp assembles at the lodge," Miss Tina said. "Tomorrow night we'll all meet at the lodge and then hike to the prairie field. There's a circle of logs to sit on, and a ton of wood stacked up in the center for a bonfire. At first, we just stay quiet, watch the fire, and listen to the night sounds. Then, when the flames die down, we roast marshmallows on willow sticks and have a sing-a-long."

That night, I climbed up to my bunk, punch-drunk on the strange and wonderful newness of camp.

"G'night, Muskrats," I said in sing-song.

"G'night, your damn self," Cherry barked. Sometime before dawn, she got up and swiped the tube of toothpaste from Vickie's shelf.

The following night, the whole camp gathered at the prairie field. A lozenge moon had breasted the horizon, bathing the prairie field in milky light. I sat between Cherry and Miss Tina on a log felled before my parents were born. The bonfire was massive. Licks of flame sent sparks high in the air. Everybody sang "Kumbaya" and swayed in time to the music. Everybody except Cherry.

"You'll sing along now, won't you?" Miss Tina begged Cherry. "The Kookaburra song's next."

Cherry cracked a twig and tossed the pieces at the fire. Refusing to sing was one thing, but refusing to sway botched up our whole section. Each time I swayed, I clunked Cherry's shoulder, and she gave me a hard shove in the opposite direction.

Miss Tina persisted. "Cherry, honey, would you lead 'Greensleeves?'"

Cherry sang her own version:

> *Alas, my glove, you doo-doo me wrong*
> *To piss me off discourteously,*
> *For I have loved you in hell so long*
> *Delighting in your nudity.*

The camp director rolled his eyes. Two girls in Beaver Unit burst out laughing. Miss Tina sighed. "Well, I'll sing it then," she said.

> *Alas, Cherry, you do me wrong,*
> *To cast me off discourteously.*
> *For I have loved you well and long,*
> *Delighting in your company.*

> *Muskrats are all my joy*
> *Oh Muskrats are my delight,*
> *Muskrats have a heart of gold,*
> *Including my lady, Cherry.*

I glanced at Cherry. The fire had died to embers. I couldn't be sure, but I thought I saw her eyes puddled with tears.

By Wednesday morning, after hiking sun-baked trails and braiding lanyards in a stifling craft tent, after riding aromatic horses through sweltering meadows and bedding down in a cabin doing business as an oven, I was in need of a good hosing-off. Like every other camper, I had shunned the slimy, spider-infested showers and, like every other kid that summer of 1955, I had been denied even a quick dip in the swimming pool.

At the sound of reveille, Vickie and Mary Kay shuffled off to the latrine. From below, I heard Cherry groan. "Lord, it's hot as Hades."

I jumped down and side-stepped along the aisle. I'd almost made it to the shelves when my arm brushed against Cherry. She shoved me away, and then sat cross-legged on her bunk and cupped her chin in her hands. She looked diminished, defeated.

"Damn the heat. Damn the mess hall food. Damn the DAMN mosquitoes and June bugs!"

I pulled on my last pair of clean socks, hopping on one foot and then the other, trying not to touch Cherry. Without warning she jumped up, planted her fists on her skinny hips, and shouted:

"You stink!"

What? I smell?

Cherry snatched an uncapped tube from Mary Kay's shelf, yanked up my arm, and slathered deodorant in the hollow underneath.

It was cool and wet, a new sensation. I was mortified.

"Girl," she said, stepping back and laughing, "you needed fumigat'n."

The idea that Cherry would take offense at my lack of personal hygiene struck me as pretty funny, too. I wrapped my arms around her bony shoulders and we laughed until our bellies ached.

For the rest of the week, Cherry and I were the best of friends. On square dance night, I picked Cherry to be my do-si-do partner. When we sang "If You're Happy and You Know it Clap Your Hands," Cherry smacked my knee to make the clapping sound.

The week was soon over. On the final morning, I packed my craft projects and award badges, and took out my autograph book. All the Muskrats signed it. Miss Tina, too.

After lunch, the entire camp assembled in the quadrangle and sang "This Land is Your Land." I hugged Miss Tina and promised to come back next year. I wanted to live at camp, like Cherry, wanted to braid lanyards and ride horses and shoot arrows at targets forever. I wanted to sit next to my new friend and sing "Kumbaya."

Mom was standing beside the DeSoto's open door. On the way down the gravel drive, I hung my head out the window, looking for Cherry. Finally, I spotted her. She was sitting on bald dirt by the flag pole. Mr. Franklin's beagle was curled in her lap and she was stroking its head. I called out, but she wouldn't look up.

That night, I wrote to her at camp.

Dear Cherry,

I had a super-duper time at camp. Remember the trail ride when your horse plopped a big one (ha-ha) and my horse trotted through it? I hope we see each other soon. You will always be my friend.

Love,

Grace Townsend

At the end of the summer, Cherry sent a reply.

> Hi New Girl,
> I rember you. You was my only frend.
> Love, Cherry.
> PS: My horse couldn't help it.

I sprinted out to our backyard. Mom was pinning towels to the line. "I got a letter from Cherry, my camp friend," I said, handing her a clothespin. My mother looked at the note, and then, with a frown, studied the return address:

Pruitt-Igoe, 2300 Cass Ave., Saint Louis, Missouri

"Can I have Cherry for a sleep-over? Can I?"

"No, and don't pester, Grace."

"I know why," I shouted, "because she's colored!"

I ran to the patio, flopped onto a wicker chair, and buried my face in my hands. I heard my mother flap a damp towel in the air. When I looked up, she was pinning it to the line.

Remembering that afternoon now, through the long lens of maturity, I suspect my mother's decision well thought out, more than it seemed.

Pruitt-Igoe was a huge public housing project, one in which misguided urban planners shoveled the poorest or the poor into a cluster of high-rise buildings. The apartments were purposefully small, lacked air-conditioning, and accessed by elevators that stopped only on every other floor. The idea was that the occupants would congregate in congenial, neighborly fashion outside the confines of their apartments, but the reality was they had to walk up or down dark stairwells to get home, to empty trash, do laundry, go anywhere. And the stairwells of Pruitt-Igoe were perilous, home turf for rapists, slashers, thieves, and worse.

We had no idea whether Cherry's parents owned a car. If I invited her and then found out she had no transportation, I couldn't take back the invitation; that would have been cruel. My father would have had to drive down to Pruitt-Igoe and venture into one of the crime-infested towers to get her, which wouldn't have been safe for him, or ask Cherry to wait outside, which wouldn't have been safe for her.

I look back on my childhood—and I am not alone in this—and I remember doctors who sat at the edge of my bed, encyclopedia salesmen who wore palm tree neckties, nuns with men's names, librarians with lavender hair, movie ushers with flashlights, filling station attendants with brimmed caps. Bank tellers. Grocery clerks. To the last, they were white.

Aside from Odetta, our maid, I was unacquainted with a single person of color, except Cherry.

I never saw her again. I thought of her over the years, though, and always with gratitude. She opened my heart to a friendship that broached fierce borders and, in so doing, opened my eyes to the possibility of a color-blind world.

To this day, whenever I happen to hear "Greensleaves," a ballad whose melody was first set to sheet music in 1580 at a college in Dublin, whose lyrics were first registered that same year at a stationery company in London, a minor chord ditty based on Italian composition that supposedly refers to a woman who might—or might not— have been a future queen of the realm, to this day I think of a bone-skinny girl with trailing shoe laces, a girl named Cherry.

Flower Mountain Festival

Miao people of China

Maureen Tolman Flannery

Forget this waiting for a phone to ring.
In Yunnan province they sing for a spouse,
screech their loneliness out across the valley,
releasing high-pitched strains of pure intent.
Sharp tones of the old songs fly
like arrows of Eros to distant hills
where someone who needs a partner
might be inclined to take up the duet.

For thousands of years this has been
the way to say, I'm ready.
Words of these same courtship verses
have mated ancestors of everyone here.
And what clearer indications of affinity than this:
potential partners blend to harmonize, adjust
the sending and the listening to compatibility.

What can we learn from talking to a person:
things they have and things they've been told.
A spouse who can sing will know how to show love
and call household joy down from the mountains.

Transfiguration at Tanglewood

Gretchen Fletcher

Ozawa's mighty arms spread out like wings
to bring a symphony across the lawn.
The orchestra's broad brass and sustained strings
fling out gold stars that light the sky like dawn.
Mahler echoes out across the hills
and drops like rain from Berkshires' massive pines
down on my ears until my whole soul fills
and makes me feel as drunk as though from wine.
Our picnics packed so carefully lie shut
lest opening them would break the music's spell,
and stop the train of Mahler's powerful thought.
While in my heart the music starts to swell
like a balloon too large for me to hold.
It bursts and I become those stars of gold.

The Guitarist Playing Villa-Lobos

Sylvia Forges-Ryan

Shoulders a protective arc
      around the amber
            chords, his pale hand's mystery

above the gut and
      bone precedes the sound that lifts
            us, breathless, as though

we too might sing that gleam of
      melody, might let
            what is deepest out, might rinse

the air with something
      like this startle of bright red
      arpeggios, their

harmonies breaking like eggs,
      eliminating
            everything but our rapture

and terror, circling us like
rings inside a tree.

Piano Solo

Pat Gallant

There's an anonymity about New York City living that is accepted and, at times, even welcomed. We have privacy. We know who our neighbors are but we don't really "know" them. We can be sure no one visits unannounced.

Christmas time here embraces this anonymity. But ask any New Yorker—there's nothing quite like Christmas in New York. We may not provide the quietude of sitting around a country hearth with cushions of snow surrounding us, but we have hustle and bustle. The feeling in the air is electric.

The draw to go "downtown" to see the window displays on Fifth Avenue, along with the grand Christmas tree at Rockefeller Center, is inescapable. It holds the memories of many fine movies—more importantly—it holds the memories of people raised here; people who call this large city "home." It holds my memories. So, I venture forth with a friend, opening the album of Manhattan, this pre-Christmas evening.

My friend and I stroll along Fifth Avenue. The energy is palpable. Everyone is scurrying about, holding mounds of shopping bags. It's a cold night and the wind gives a push at our backs. Chestnuts roast on open fires, just as the song depicts. There is shoving and tugging and irritation inside the stores, as tired patrons rush to buy last-minute gifts from stores open late to accommodate them. Outside, shoppers crane necks over crowds to see the window displays. Others are racing along, trying to finish their shopping before the stores close. It's nearing 10 P.M. I'm ready to call it a night but it's impossible to find an empty taxi, so we continue walking along Fifth Avenue, amongst the anonymous crowds.

The pushing and shoving inside the stores has now moved outside. As the wind picks up, snow begins to fall and the temperature drops. Everyone is trying to out-maneuver everyone else to get a taxi. Drained shoppers cut one another off at the sight of a taxi whose light indicates it is empty.

A somewhat bedraggled looking man, pushing a small, weather-beaten piano on wheels, stops on the sidewalk, along the curb. He pulls a folding chair from atop the piano which he deftly opens up and plunks down on.

Little surprises us in Manhattan. He is winded but determined. He places an empty cup on top of the piano and begins to play. I watch as his ungloved fingers slide along the keys. Then, I look down at my fingers, frozen and aching from the cold, and I wonder how he can play with such ease. "Silent Night" fills the air. People stop. Then more people. A man in the crowd begins singing. Then a woman. Then another person and another. Strangers join hands and sway back and forth to the music. No one jumps to grab the lone, empty taxi that rides by. Soon everyone is holding hands and singing, "Silent night, Holy night..." A policeman smiles and looks the other way, ignoring the hard fact that street peddling is illegal. The man's cup, once empty, now runneth over. It is, after all, the Christmas season. A few more carols are sung and when the man finishes playing, the crowd disburses as everyone, once again, begins his or her fade back into anonymity. But something magical has transpired. I am left feeling with full certainty that for those of us who shared in this special moment, "all is calm, all is bright."

Sam's Song

William Grady

I've become accustomed to visiting Sam every day. I take the midtown bus to the end of the line, and walk the last four blocks. Most days are just like today, and I arrive without remembering how I got here. It would be easy to skip a day or two, maybe take in a movie, but Sam is always waiting. Today, I have new music and he's going to love the kettle drums.

My backpack is loaded with the usual stuff. The foot-long sandwich is already cut in the middle, in case Sam wants half. The Nicholas Sparks book I'm reading for the third time sits in the front pouch, where I can see the red beads on my American Indian bookmark. Sam confessed to removing the "Made in China" sticker before dropping it into a book I was reading.

The security staff waves me in, as usual, and I skip up the stairwell to the third floor. At the end of the corridor is room 309, exactly ninety-two green floor tiles from the stairway. My rubber soles squish out an echo; the only sound on this floor. It can be eerie if you let the silence get to you. Sometimes I count the squishes along with the tiles. Half-way down the corridor I pass an empty desk. It is the nurses' station, which by law, must be occupied around the clock. In practice, it seldom is.

I slide the backpack off and push the door open. "Hi, Sam. What's up?" He stares but doesn't speak. "I'm glad all your visitors have left. I didn't bring enough food for a big crowd. Guess what I brought for dinner.......go ahead, guess."

Sam doesn't answer and I know there haven't been any other visitors in this room for a very long time. Sam's mom came faithfully for a while. Now she's back home in Seattle and occasionally emails to ask if there has been any change.

I clear the dining table, which doubles during the day as a window sill. "Don't even look over here," I say. "You didn't want to know....remember?"

"Okay, it's tuna again, your favorite.........hey, let's make a pact okay? The first thing we're going to do when you get out of here is go for a T-bone steak. That's the best, right? A T-bone? I'm never going to have a cold sandwich for dinner again. Are you laughing at me?" I look intently into Sam's eyes. "No? Okay, don't you dare laugh at me."

As I eat I scan the room wishing something, anything, was different than the day before. It never is, and I vow again to bring in some pictures.

"Sam, I've got an idea. Let's paint this room. No, seriously. I bet they wouldn't even notice. We could do one wall at a time. What do you think? I know you like green, maybe we'll do one wall green. Better yet, I'll bring in some swatches tomorrow and we'll pick out a color together."

I finish the sandwich, roll up the wrapper and throw it in the trash bin. It lands on top of yesterday's wrapper, and the one from the day before. "Doesn't anyone clean this place?" I ask. "I'm going to tell them you're quite dissatisfied with the service." I chuckle to make light of it, but am not pleased.

It's almost time to sit with Mr. Sparks. By now, the last four chapters hold no surprises. Far too much of life has become sadly predictable. But today I brought something completely *unpredictable*. My new ear-buds will be a change for Sam and perfect for tonight's therapy.

"Sam, I have different music tonight. You're going to freak." I turn on my iPod and set it on Sam's pillow.

"You know how Dr. Weirdo suggested music you were familiar with? Well, so far you haven't liked that very much. So now, he says to try something very different; something you've never heard before. I found just the thing."

I wait politely for a response, but Sam says nothing.

"It's got a funny name, sounds German to me. First word is 'also.' Can you say that? Also?.....No? Well the next word is Sprach. I looked it up. It means 'spoken,' and that's odd because there are no words. I'm serious. Don't look at me that way."

After selecting the right song I pick up the white ear-buds and show them to Sam. "I read that this music was the soundtrack for a movie, 2001: *Space Odyssey*. Don't know what that is. But they always used it in Las Vegas to introduce Elvis Presley. I know....Elvis, right? Guess that means your mom would like it......The full name? Wait, let me check....It says *Also Sprach Zarathustra*, or something like that. I listened to it last night. The bass blew my head off."

With that I place the place the buds in Sam's ears and start the music. When I sink down into the rocker, my shoes slip off easily. After opening to page 186, I remove the beaded marker and reach to place it on a side table. Wait.....something happened.

I leap to my feet and stand over Sam. I swear something moved. Nothing ever moves in this room. I stare intently. No hair is out of place. The headphones are still on, arms folded. Oh, there it is!!!

An eye twitched. OH MY GOD. AN EYE TWITCHED. "SAM....SAM." Nothing! In an instant I'm out the door, yelling for help. I slap the empty desk as I sprint to the stairs and head to the first floor.

At the front desk, Joe, the security guard, and Emma, a night nurse, are making small talk. I yell, "Sam twitched." They look at each other, but don't move. "Hurry," I say. "Sam twitched."

Joe asks, "What's that mean?"

Emma says, "Happens all the time. It's just a reflex."

"No," I yell. "I've been here every day. It's never happened before."

Again they look at each other. Emma says, "I'll come up."

I head back up to Room 309, and burst in, ready for excitement. Sam twitched, the nurse is coming, and something is happening. For some reason, it feels necessary to put my shoes on and stand back out of the nurse's way. I smile at Sam. "T-bone.....I promise."

Emma saunters in with the urgency of a postal clerk. Her bored expression irritates me. Sam doesn't move a muscle. "Do it again, Sam," I yell out.

After a cursory exam she turns to leave. "It was just a reflex," she says, and closes the door behind her. For a minute I stare at the door, expecting it to fly open at any second and reveal a team of specialists, with machines and monitors. I wonder what Sam's mother is doing right now in Seattle. I wonder what I'll say to her when I call.

But the door doesn't open. No rescue is imminent. There is no miracle to record. I look at Sam and wait for another twitch, but none comes. I reach to find my book on the floor without taking my eyes off Sam. The deep despair that accompanied the original prognosis is back. "Keep trying, Sam. I'll be here."

One bud had slipped out of place and I slide it back while looking into Sam's eyes. *Also Sprach Zarathustra*, I yell out, "and don't scare me this time." I hit *play* and crank up the volume so the bass is audible, even through the headphones.

I hear the boom of kettle drums and pray Sam hears them, too.

⋮

66

⋮

Lake Geneva, 2001

Mary Ann Grzych

Barbra Streisand was singing "Walking in a Winter Wonderland" when Pam came into the house at noon on Christmas Day. Barely stamping the snow off her Prada boots, she marched across the carpet leaving wet tracks as though daring her sister to say something.

"Winter wonderland, my ass. It's terrible out there—snow everywhere. Half the streets in Chicago aren't plowed yet. I almost got stuck getting out of Wrigleyville. Why do I pay taxes if those lazy city workers can't keep the streets clean on Christmas?" she grumbled, not even bothering to say hello.

Pam dumped her snow-covered cashmere coat on Trish's new bedspread along with her Coach purse and leather gloves. Reaching up, she lightly brushed her short, stylishly cut, blond hair in an effort to dislodge the few snowflakes brave enough to land there. A month ago, her hair had been shoulder-length and auburn.

"Nice hair, Sis," Trish said.

"I needed a change and short is easy."

They were no longer kids, but it was obvious that Pam still wanted to make herself look different from Trish. Today she wore a sleek, winter-white pantsuit. Trish had an apron over plain brown slacks and white tee top. The only thing distinguishing it from her usual work clothes as a gym teacher was the appliqué of Santa smiling from his sleigh.

Pam could change her hair and clothes, but nothing would change the reality that they were both five-foot-six, and had inherited their mother's slender frame, clear ivory complexion and electric-blue eyes. Being Trish's identical twin had irked Pam most of her life. Throughout high school and college in the 1980s, Pam had been a cheerleader for the football team and had worn whatever was considered cute and trendy at the time.

She hung around with the 'in crowd'.

Trish had been a swim leader with wet hair hanging limply down her back almost every day, and had preferred slacks and comfortable tops similar to what she wore today. They didn't have the wardrobe problem that lots of sisters do; they *never* wore each other's clothes.

Their mom had said the house often seemed a battlefield, especially during their teen years. She couldn't understand how her twins could be so different. Pam's answer was, "We just are. People need to accept it!" Some of the light dimmed in their mother's eyes on days like that. Pam seemed not to notice, but Trish did.

Trish was optimistic. Pam, always pessimistic, looked at life as something to be endured rather than relished. Today, true to form, she had complained about the streets that weren't plowed, instead of being thankful for those that were.

"I need to get back to making dinner," Trish said, walking out of the bedroom.

Sniffing the air as she passed the kitchen, Pam sniped, "The house reeks of turkey. Did you burn it? Aren't Bret and Shirley supposed to be here already?" Not waiting for answers she continued to the front room, adding, "I didn't bring my packages in. Bret can do that when he gets here. How'd he manage to get Christmas off?"

"An older fireman changed days with him so that he could be home with the kids."

The fact that their brother had two small children and a trunk full of their own things to bring in wouldn't have entered Pam's ad-exec mind. The muscles of Trish's neck tightened as her temples began to ache. Closing her eyes, she took a deep breath, slowly lowered her head and silently sighed, vowing not to let Pam's chronic complaints ruin Christmas again. *I'll be as sweet as the pumpkin pie I baked for dessert, no matter how sharp her tongue.*

The first Christmas after their mother died, three years ago, Trish had invited everyone to spend the holiday in Lake Geneva. Dad was especially grateful. Bret and Shirley with one-year-old Ronnie were also relieved that their family tradition would continue. Shirley's parents in California rarely came to the Midwest in winter. Pam, however, had begun a pattern of finding something to complain about.

"I miss those elegant touches Mom put on the table. Would it hurt to use her Waterford candlesticks?" Pam snapped that first Christmas. "After all, she left them to *you!*"

"If you have candles to put in, get them from the china cabinet," Trish retorted. "I can't remember everything."

"I'll bring some next year."

"You do that." The rest of the day had been tense.

"Where's Pa?" Pam hollered from the front room. "With all that snow on his car, he must have spent the night. Aren't you embarrassed to have that old jalopy in your driveway?"

"He did. We went to candlelight service at church last night. It was beautiful. The choir sang some of Dad's favorites." Trish heard an annoyed "'Humph," but ignored it along with Pam's snide remark about his car. "Dad's in the spare room. He had some last minute wrapping to do," she answered knowing full well he had finished that chore last night. He had, in fact, skedaddled with her Golden Lab, Belmont, right on his heels, the minute he saw Pam's car in the driveway. She had that effect on people, even her own father. Pam insisted on calling him Pa, even though she knew that he hated it.

Trish remembered Dad's reaction when it started a few years ago. "'Pa' makes me feel like an old geezer in a movie I once saw," he confided. "She can't stand my plaid shirts and jeans, but I've been done with suits since I retired from the bank when your mom got sick.

"I could just ignore it when she does that, like Mom and I did when you kids tried using our first names when you were little. But it's not worth a battle. She's not little anymore and it makes her look more foolish than me," he'd said.

"I'm starving. When are we going to eat?" Pam called from the front room, jolting Trish back to today.

"Dinner will be served when Bret and Shirley get here," Trish said. "They called around ten when they were leaving. Should be here soon."

・・・
69
・・・

The day had started off badly for Bret and Shirley. The Christmas Eve snowfall had continued into the morning. Bret would have to shovel the sidewalk before leaving Chicago's Southwest side for Lake Geneva.

Three-month-old Jessica had spent a colicky night waking several times, knees drawn up in pain, crying even after Shirley picked her up. They had barely drifted back to sleep, for the third time, when four-year-old Ronnie woke them shouting excitedly, "Mom, Dad, come look. Santa was here!" No one slept after that.

Getting Ronnie ready for the trip was almost impossible once he saw the toys. Shirley finally bribed him saying, "You can take the carpenter set along to show Grandpa, if you put it down now and come eat breakfast."

Bret sat by the tree, still in pajamas. His long legs were splayed in a "v" as he put the plastic tools back into Ronnie's new carpenter set.

A smile crossed his face. Motioning Shirley over, he whispered, "When I was his age I got a set just like this. I tried to saw the leg off the dining room table Christmas Day. Dad stained the scratch marks, but you can still see them if you know where to look. I'll show you when we get to Trish's."

"I'm sorry I said he could take it along."

"Don't worry. Dad remembers. He'll keep an eye on Ronnie and the saw." Bret's dark eyes twinkled with almost as much excitement as Ronnie's. "I'm really looking forward to Christmas Day by the lake." He'd retrieved his old sled from the garage loft, sanded the rust from the runners, waxed them, and promised Ronnie that they'd sled down the hill onto the lake after dinner.

Shirley wiped a dribble of milk from Jessie's chin, then shifted her up to burp. "Do you want breakfast?" she asked Bret.

"I'll take mine to go," he answered, putting on his jacket and grabbing two Krispie Cremes from the open box on the counter. He left the kids to Shirley while he shoveled, then packed the Corolla's trunk with shopping bags of Christmas presents, the carpenter set, Jessie's oversized diaper bag, the porta-crib, a bag of play clothes for Ronnie to wear sledding and, of course, the sled. The trunk barely closed.

By the time she had Ronnie and Jess ready to go, Shirley's new, red silk blouse was wrinkled and its tail hung out of her navy gabardine slacks. "I feel like a frump," she said dejectedly to Bret. "Your sister, Pam, will be dressed to the teeth and looking at me like a refugee just off the boat."

"She'll be over-dressed for a family dinner and looking down at all of us. Just ignore her," he said giving Shirley a loving pat on the derriere. "The car's packed. Let me know when you're ready for me to put the kids in their seats."

"I hope Ronnie won't need a bathroom along the way. There probably aren't any open except the Oasis on I-294. Maybe you should take a jar along, just in case," Shirley said.

"Nah, if worse comes to worse, I can pull over and let him whiz on the side of the road," Bret laughed from the kitchen.

Ten minutes later they were on their way, listening to Christmas carols and hoping Jessie would fall asleep. No such luck. They had just passed the O'Hare Oasis when Jessie's fussing turned into full-blown wailing drowning out "Jingle Bells." Her problem soon became apparent. The odor was unmistakable.

"Phew, she stinks!" Ronnie said, holding his nose and begging to move to the front seat away from his sister.

"Maybe I can change her if you find a shoulder wide enough to pull over safely," Shirley said.

"Sorry, the diaper bag's in the trunk, behind all the presents."

"Why on earth did you put it *there*?"

"You said to make sure the presents didn't get squashed, so I put them in last," he said sheepishly. "I didn't think that we'd need it until we got to Trish's."

"Just like a man," said Shirley, a hint of lighthearted teasing in her voice. "It doesn't smell any better up here," she said turning her head toward the back seat. "You'll have to stay where you are, Ronnie." By the time they had reached the Wisconsin State line, both kids were asleep and the snow had stopped. Things were looking up.

～ ✿ ✿ ～

Trish had just put the turkey onto Mom's holiday platter and was envisioning herself tomorrow night. Company gone, she'd sit in front of the fireplace, feet on the hassock. The plate on her lap would hold a savory sandwich piled high with leftover turkey, Mayo, crisp lettuce and a thin slice of tomato as a cup of coffee steamed at her side. Johnny Mathis' velvet voice would be singing "Chestnuts roasting on an open fire..." in the background as she enjoyed the Christmas tree with all its special decorations and the memories they evoked.

Pam broke the spell when she hollered from her perch on the sofa, "They're finally here."

Wiping her hands on her apron, Trish tapped on the guest room door. "Bret and Shirley and the kids are here, Dad," she said then headed for the front room. Dad followed closely behind. Belmont beat them both to the door, his tail wagging excitedly as he licked Ronnie's face, creating squeals of joy.

"Stop that and take your boots off, Ronnie," Shirley ordered bending down to remove her own. Dad was pulling Belmont off Ronnie when Bret came in the door, a squawking Jessie in his arms. He handed her to Trish who promptly plopped her on Pam's lap then turned to help Ronnie with his jacket zipper.

"She smells bad," Ronnie announced. Pam's face screwed up in distaste as she held baby Jess at arm's length.

"I'll change her as soon as Bret digs the diaper bag out from the back of the trunk," Shirley said, flashing him a look.

"You need to bring the packages from my car, too," Pam ordered their kid brother. "And be careful not to mess up the bows."

Shirley took time to hug Trish and Dad before rescuing a howling Jessie from Pam's outstretched grip. Ronnie, free of his coat, was chasing Belmont into the kitchen.

"I'd better protect the turkey from those two," Trish said heading toward the kitchen. "Use the spare room for Jess. Dinner's on in twenty minutes if someone helps," she added, inclining her head toward the front room. Pam didn't take the hint. She was used to delegating, not doing.

"Tell me what you need done," Shirley said a few minutes later. She handed a now smiling, sweet smelling Jessie to Bret. He'd finished lugging in all the paraphernalia from the Carolla's overstuffed trunk and delivered Pam's packages—to her—bows intact.

"Just take the dishes to the table as I fill them. And *you* can get out of the kitchen," Trish said slapping Bret's free hand away from the turkey platter.

⸺ ✤ ⸺

Dinner went surprisingly well until the very end when Ronnie spilled his milk onto Pam's designer pants. "Shit," she said, jumping up, nearly falling over Belmont. "This is the last time I'll dress up for dinner until these kids are twenty-one."

Everyone was stunned. For a moment the only sound was Oscar Peterson's piano rendition of *Winter Wonderland* coming from the stereo until Dad's voice cut the silence. "Pamela!"

There was no mistaking the tone. Pam knew she had gone too far even before she saw Ronnie's tears. She had to fix it.

"Don't worry, Ronnie," she said patting his curly black hair, "I'm just kidding. I once knocked over a whole pitcher of milk. This is nothing compared to *that* mess. Mom gave me a big hug. Can I give you a hug, Ronnie?" she asked, reaching out. Head down, Ronnie stepped forward as he felt the pressure of his Dad's hand on his back.

"Why don't you go sledding with us," Bret asked his sister. "You can borrow some jeans from Trish."

Hesitating briefly, her index finger across her lips, Pam said, "God, I can't remember the last time I went sledding. It must be twenty years ago. We were just kids. Would that be OK with you, Ronnie?"

"Sure," Ronnie replied after getting a nod of approval from his dad.

"We'll have dessert later," Trish said as she and Pam went to her bedroom to find some sledding clothes.

Fifteen minutes later, Bret, Ronnie and Pam headed out the door, with Belmont close behind jumping and barking, as excited as Ronnie was.

"She always did find a way to get out of doing the dishes," Dad said, laughing, as Pam flew down the hill toward the lake on Bret's old sled, her arms and legs entwined around Ronnie, both of them yelling, "Wheeeee!"

Walk with Music

Nancy J. Heggem

From south to north, country villages,
cows in their meadows, sheep on the hills,
narrow trails and sandy Atlantic beaches
this woman, secure and mature at fifty,
steps on the path with only her camera,
and music, as walking companions.

On the fourth day of the fourth month, 2004,
when it was 4 AM in Quebec City, Canada,
Monique, from Quebec, took her first step
a 2,000 kilometer solo walk across France.

Her pictures capture
flowers sparkling with dew
hedge rows, rose covered walls
grape vines sprouting, trees heavy with fruit
shots of laughing grandmas, bike riding boys
cottages and country churches, signs at crossroads
clouds gathering in April sky
brilliant golden sunshine in May
summer sunsets of July.

Just pictures and music, capture the day
reviewed each night. Off with boots,
rest in bed, tent or beach.
On the little music machine,
her favorites, old friends,
play, sing, rhythm of the walk.

The Red Ribbon Karaoke

Timmothy J. Holt

The AIDS blues offers no redemption
so I no longer hum the tune,
lip-synch the words,
though the lyrics are memorized.

Grace was bestowed and forgotten
from an audience who lost interest.
Let a new generation be heard
in a song of their own,

let them dance a tangled tango,
mine shall remain a ballad
slow, romantic, an epic poem
of a love affair I've accepted.

Daydreaming

Timmothy J. Holt

Sitting on the bank
she hears an invisible band,

holds an invisible hand,
head on an invisible shoulder.

Her eyes overflow with desire,
but, arthritic legs say sit old woman.

She dredges up a tune for the river
to flow its slow dance,

a waltz would be her choice,
but water over sunken boulders

foam with desire
in their exotic tango.

With a cane she rises,
brushes away the dust,

a stone in hand
she skips across

water, where waves
solicit her private dance.

A Summer Sound in a Summer without End

Jane Hoogestraat

Staring too long at the same waves, watching a Cessna
notch a wind current, then correct, as a voice might
catch, right itself, an almost indistinguishable stutter,
I realize a pilot is practicing, arcing briefly over the Atlantic,
circling back to a grassy air field before climbing again,
that the wing makes it slight dip the same place each time,
a riffle in a sail that won't flatten, a chill never quite shaken,
how the ocean darkens when you have stared too long
across the sunlit tide, then turn your gaze elsewhere.

The shore seems meditative today, a point in the distance
where a high surf mists against the trees, two figures
walking, taking a long time to arrive, an inward focus
visible everywhere, people reading against the glare,
even the joy of children muted by the sea, while the plane
masters everything, it seems, save the one small turn,
like a gull checked by wind, like moments in Satie,
Mahler, that will never resolve, wayfaring stories
we will live with, stories without endings, ever.

Silent Night in the Barn Quarter

Julie A. Jacob

It was the last day of the magical winter journey to Germany. Our tour guide, Raphael, a droll Italian-born British historian who lived in Berlin, had invited us to his apartment for a farewell dinner. He was being rather mysterious about it, but we, the band of twenty-two hardy travellers from Wisconsin, knew that the evening he was planning would be wonderful. It had been that kind of trip.

Going on the Wisconsin Public Radio-sponsored vacation had been an impulsive decision. As I drowsed in bed on a September morning, listening to WPR, I heard by chance an advertisement for the trip. Christmas markets, classical music concerts, and museum excursions—it sounded enchanting.

"This is the trip I told you about," I said to my dad a few days later, handing him my laptop opened to the WPR travel page.

"This sounds great," my dad said, scanning the information on the Christmas market in Nuremberg, the Bach Museum in Leipzig, and the concert at the Wilhelm Kaiser Memorial Church in Berlin. "I want you to go and have fun. I'll be fine."

So I signed up, never dreaming that by the time I departed three months later, my father would be gone, taken by brain cancer in just six days after years of struggling with vascular disease.

I almost cancelled the trip. How could I go a mere four weeks after the funeral, when my grief was as raw as the November wind and my sister and I were struggling to absorb the loss of our last surviving parent? Yet my father had wanted me to go. It would be the last vacation I would ever take that he knew about.

So I left for O'Hare Airport on a December evening after an early dinner with my sister and brother-in-law. They waved good-bye as I boarded the airport shuttle bus; we smiled and tried to act more cheerful than we felt. Thirteen hours later, I landed in Munich. Raphael and Melanie, a gentle woman who hosted a WPR folk-music program, were waiting for us beyond the customs checkpoint. It was an eclectic group that clustered around our guide and host. The travellers included a neurologist, a piano teacher, a nurse, a retired judge, and several professors. One couple from Milwaukee, Pete and Mary, played the mandolin and guitar. They carried their instruments on their backs as we traveled on trains and buses from Munich to Berlin, and they played folk songs in the hotel lobbies in the evenings.

My fellow travellers were years older than I; most had lost one or both parents. "My dad passed away four weeks ago, and my mom died eight years ago," was all I had to say and my new friends engulfed me with sympathy. A murmured "I'm sorry" as we followed Rafe down a cobblestone street, a "how are you doing?" as we waited for the train to Leipzig, or an exchange of parental loss stories over a dinner of dumplings and sauerkraut showed that they understood in a way that friends who still had both their parents could not.

The trip was brilliant. Rafe, who had a master's degree in history from Oxford, gave us mini-lectures every day on German history, art, and music. It was like attending a graduate seminar in European history, but one with excellent food and good wine, terrific company and no papers to write.

Two other women traveling solo befriended me, and in Nuremberg we strolled though the *Weihnachtsmarkt* one night as we sipped *glühwein* and nibbled on sweet almonds. Two enormous, brightly lit fir trees, as beautiful as the magical Christmas tree in *The Nutcracker*, framed the entrance to an enormous stone church. In front of the trees, beneath a red-and-white-striped awning, a choir sang "O Come All Ye Faithful." The next day the group toured St. Sebaldus's Church, which had been destroyed during World War II and rebuilt as a monument to peace. As we explored the empty church, gazing at stained glass windows and Veit Stoss wooden sculptures, an organist practiced for an upcoming concert, as though she were playing just for us.

Our next stop was Leipzig, where we attended a classical music concert in the angular *Gendwandhaus*. The musicians in the Leipzig Orchestra played Mahler's First Symphony with such intensity that they trembled in their seats. The following evening we slid quietly into the wooden pews in the 700-year-old St. Thomas Church, where Bach had served as music director for twenty-five years, and listened to a choir of young singers perform pieces by Bach, Bruckner, and Mendelssohn.

On we journeyed to Berlin, where we took a day trip to Potsdam, the 19th-centruy playground of the German aristocracy. We toured the snow-dusted grounds of the summer palace of King Frederick the

Great. It was dusk and near the palace grounds a stately windmill was silhouetted against a rose-colored sky. Only the sweet notes of a flute broke the winter stillness as a musician dressed in 18th-century garb stood by the palace's entrance and played one of the king's own compositions.

The new sights and busy schedule and friendly company kept my knot of grief at bay, at least until the evenings when I was alone in my hotel room and plugged in my cell phone to charge it, saddened that I no longer needed to call my father.

Rafe wryly called Berlin a "massive mind mess" because of its complex and sorrowful past. I had thought it would be a city gray and brooding, like the metropolis in *Wings of Desire* that the pony-tailed angels soberly observed as they stood on the edges of rooftops, hands shoved in the pockets of their long wool coats. Instead, I discovered a charming city of good restaurants, magnificent museums and an enormous park. A double line of bricks embedded in the ground wound through the city like a scar, marking the location of the wall that had once split the city.

On the final day of the trip, we had a few free hours in the afternoon. I slipped away to wander through a Christmas market in the *Gendarmenmarkt*. Rows of white tents, draped with garlands of white lights, filled a square bordered by the French and German cathedrals and the Berlin Concert House. Feathery snowflakes tumbled down from the sky, covering the trees and ground with a white quilt. Inside the tents, vendors sold wooden toys, wool scarves, and delicate ornaments. One vendor sold photographs of angel statues. I flipped through the basket of pictures, hoping that one would provide some comfort, but the stone angels' impassive expressions offered no solace.

I went back outside, where the air smelled pleasantly of spices, chocolate and sizzling wurst. I bought a *glühwein* and a bag of cinnamon almonds and walked to the center of the square. The glow from green and red lights warmed the white marble Friedrich Schiller statue. Behind Schiller, on a stage in trimmed with evergreens and white lights, a jazz band improbably played a honky-tonk version of "Ain't Misbehavin'." The *glühwein* warmed me to my toes. I felt nearly content, but I so wanted to call my father to say *Hi, dad, I'm at a Christmas market in Berlin. It's beautiful. Mom would have loved it.*

The next day, I reflected, it was back to Wisconsin and my father's silent house, filled with fifty years of memories, and a life without my father's love. The knot of grief tightened in my stomach.

Reluctantly, I left the market and took the U-Bahn back to the sleek hotel, all blond wood and glass, where we were staying. Rafe, who was busy preparing for our feast, had instructed us to gather in the lobby at 5:30 and take the subway to Alexanderplatz. We met in the lobby, chattering in anticipation, and crossed the street to the Markisches Museum U-Bahn stop, where we descended the steps to the platform and boarded the crowded subway. We got off two stops later and stepped into a winter wonderland. The trees were wrapped in deep blue lights. Sparkling white lights shaped into giant snowflakes danced on wires strung across the streets. Amber lights glowed from the wooden booths of yet another Christmas market. People hurried past, bundled in down coats and scarves, their boots crunching on the snow. The air vibrated with music, laughter, and car horns.

Rafe was waiting for us at the U-Bahn entrance, lanky and boyish and ever so British in his tweed coat and a scarf wrapped jauntily around his neck. He was lugging an enormous suitcase filled, he said, with wine and water for our meal. We followed him across the square, stepping carefully on the icy walk. We crossed Prenzlauer Allee and walked to the Weinmeisterstrasse U-Bahn stop, where we turned right and followed Rafe down a narrow, dark street. He ushered us into the foyer of an old apartment building. The green walls were covered with strange graffiti—cats and space aliens and hearts— that had been drawn by the artists who had lived there until the neighborhood—the *Scheuenenviertel*, the Barn Quarter—became too fashionable for them to afford. Through a glass door at the back, I saw a courtyard, empty except for a few fat-tired bicycles clustered together like sheep and covered with puffy clumps of snow.

We followed Rafe up three flights of stairs, carrying folding chairs that he had retrieved from the storage room. At the landing, a woman with coppery curls and merry brown eyes greeted us at an open door. "Welcome," she said in Italian-accented English. "I'm Sofia." She and her husband, Luis, were catering the meal.

We slipped off our shoes in the hallway. The apartment was long and narrow with high ceilings and hardwood floors. Rafe removed his coat with a flourish. Instead of his baggy wool sweater, he wore a white dress shirt, a black bow tie, and a scarlet cummerbund. He ushered us to his bedroom, which was serving as the makeshift dining room. Floor-to-ceiling bookshelves crammed with books on Germany history, art history, religious history, and Renaissance poetry bordered the walls. Tall windows, framed in white-painted wood, overlooked the courtyard. One window was ajar to let in the cool night air. A door laid across two sawhorses formed a temporary table.

We arranged the chairs and set out the bottles of wine and water. Sofia and Luis hurried in and out carrying enormous platters and bowls of food: gleaming black olives, warm bread, bruschetta, a caprese salad of succulent tomatoes and delicate mozzarella cheese, tender ham medallions, and a fluffy lasagna. The conversation and wine flowed like the River Spree. Rafe dashed around, smiling and teasing us gently as he refilled our glasses.

We asked Sofia her story. She was from New Jersey, she said, the daughter of an American mother and Italian father, but had been raised in Florence. She had moved to Berlin years before and had started a catering business with Luis, her Brazilian husband.

After we could not eat another bite, we helped clear the dishes, dismantle the table and rearrange the chairs in a ragged circle. It was time for the evening's entertainment. A balding, stocky man with a red beard, dressed in a black floral print silk kimono, entered the room. A dark-haired, wiry man wearing a sport coat and carrying a keyboard followed him.

Rafe introduced the kimono-wearing man. His name was George, and he was a friend who performed cabaret music. His accompanist, Markus, was a jazz musician from Hamburg. Before he began, we asked George for *his* story. He was a playwright from New Zealand who became stranded in Berlin on his way from Auckland to Amsterdam in 2001 and had never left. He performed cabaret songs from 1920-era Berlin as his contribution to preserving the city's colorful past.

Rafe dimmed the lights and lit candles. As George sang songs of love, lust and longing in his clear tenor voice, I imagined dark cabarets, clouds of cigarette smoke, the clink of ice in glasses and smoldering glances between strangers who would soon be lovers. I thought about people trying to live and love and create art and music in a world about to go mad.

George sang one song and another and yet another, sipping water and wiping his forehead with a handkerchief between songs. Finally, hoarse, he could sing no more. Yet we didn't want the night to end. We were a group of friends from the United States, Great Britain, Germany, Italy, Brazil and New Zealand who had bonded into a little community this night in a bedroom in an apartment on a side street in what had once been East Berlin. We didn't want to leave. Melanie borrowed Pete's guitar. Seated on a folding chair, legs crossed, she strummed the guitar and sang a soulful tune about Mary and Jesus and Christmas Eve. We sat quietly for a moment as the last note quivered in the air. "Play a song," someone asked Pete and Mary. They obliged and performed a series of rollicking Woody Guthrie and Bob Dylan songs. These were the anthems from the college days of my fellow travelers. As they sang and clapped, I imagined them not as they were now, gray-haired and wearing bifocals and sensible sweaters, but as they had once had been: young, reckless, and brimming with passion to change the world.

We ended the evening by singing "Silent Night." Rafe searched on his laptop for the words in German. He stood by the window, balancing the MacBook in his hands, while Dora, a woman in our group, and I stood on either side of him. As Pete, Mary and Markus played the melody, we sang along with Rafe in our rusty college German. Then everyone sang the carol again, this time in English. The words "silent' "and "sleep" and "peace" filled the room, drifted out the open window, and floated like a gentle snowfall of musical notes to the courtyard below. I imagined the quarter notes and half notes blanketing the courtyard and the other apartments with the comfort of that simple song about a baby and serenity and hope. As we sang, the knot inside me loosened. *It's going to be okay*, I thought.

We were quiet for a few seconds after the last "peace." Then the moment broke, and we folded the chairs, gathered our coats, put on our shoes and descended the stairs. Rafe walked us through the hushed streets to the U-Bahn stop. The evening was over, and we now had to snatch a few hours of sleep before departing for the airport at 5 a.m. However, the serenity I had felt in the apartment stayed with me. How wonderful and strange is music, I thought. It can be heard only in the instant that it is sung or played. It can't be held in our hands nor folded in a pocket and saved. Yet it is real. It fills the air, it caresses our hearts, and it remains with us.

Sort of like love.

heard singing

Allan Johnston

the lone bird
keeps returning to the tree
to sing in the hot night

a different bird each time
yet the same sense
pervades the calling

the same tree and limb
the same spirit moving them
and I know

over what I hear
that this and every moment
is the only moment

a hot night clings to
every second

:

84

:

Dancing Queens

Amber Kemppainen

Dinner is almost ready, but we've got some time to kill. I push my daughter's hair out of the way carefully and zip up her dress. She gives me a quick grin and a kiss and dashes off to the living room in a swirl of fabric. Jordin Sparks starts blaring through the stereo. It is officially dancing time. I stand in the doorway for a minute and watch as my girls laugh, giggle, and twirl each other until they fall over. I send up a silent thank you that I can participate. It wasn't so long ago that this kind of exertion was impossible.

It started soon after my second daughter was born. Well, to be honest, I had issues before that. I counted eight times I went to the emergency room while I was pregnant with her. I wasn't quite on bed rest, but I really couldn't do a whole lot: no running, no picking up my girl, and no dancing. That's a big problem when you've got a two-year-old. We both need a lot of cuddling and there's really no easy way to explain to a toddler why mommy suddenly can't hold her.

Things were a little easier for awhile after my second daughter was born. There were the usual aches and pains and trying to get back into shape. Unfortunately, my body had other plans. The pain that had bothered me sporadically throughout my pregnancy was now a constant companion—a very unwelcome companion. Aside from a few trips to the doctor who couldn't explain what was happening, I did my best to ignore the pain. Fast-forward a few months and the pain was getting worse. What followed was a whirlwind cycle of doctor's visits, ineffective physical therapy and tears. The conclusion was unavoidable and heartbreaking. I needed a hysterectomy. Can you believe it? I was a 31-year-old mother-of-two who would never be able to have children again.

I always wanted a big family—at least four children. We tried for both our first and second children and it did take awhile both times, but I never imagined this. The problem was, as the doctors so callously explained, all my internal mommy organs were deciding to become external organs. Basically my connections inside had been stretched too far and they couldn't hold themselves in anymore. My only choice then was to take them out.

How do I describe how this felt? God only knows. I cried and prayed for a miracle and the pain only got worse. I couldn't walk too fast, sit, and forget about dancing with my girls. I could only watch them while I lay on the couch and remembered happier times. I used to pick them up and pretend we were waltzing. We twirled and mash-potatoed. Crazy disco moves were hilarious to them. We had our favorite songs that we would sing along to. And I couldn't do it anymore. I couldn't ignore it, as much as I wanted to, and God did I want to! I just couldn't.

What was I supposed to do? I couldn't become pregnant again without risking the baby. I couldn't go on like I was with the pain growing worse every day. I had to keep asking myself: do I hold out for more children, and search for a cure that several doctors already told me was hopeless? Or do I be the best mom I can be to the children I was already blessed with? Obviously I really didn't have an option. For a woman who really likes to be in control, this was my own personal Hell.

I made an appointment that got pushed back further and further. The moment of truth finally came on my 32nd birthday. I sat in the pre-op room trying not to cry. The only thing that kept me on that table was faith and hope—faith that this was the right thing to do, hope that things could only get better. Oh my goodness, would you listen to me? I wasn't trying to make this a sob story. Though, to be honest, I've shed quite a few tears writing this down. There is a happy ending to the tale of "woe is me."

It's now a few years later and I'm watching my daughters dance. We've all put on our fancy dresses. I've let my kids pick out their own, so my littlest is wearing her little mermaid costume with fairy wings and a cat's tail. My oldest is waving a wand and wearing a towel wrapped around her for an added train. I have on a dress as well. It's not as fancy as my daughter's, but they have assured me I am still "fabulous."

They call me to join them and I do. My girls squeal with joy as I swing them high in the air and dip them. We run around in circles until we get too dizzy and fall over. All the while we listen to Jordin Sparks sing "One Step at a Time" on endless repeat. It's one of our personal favorites. Though I still have my rough days where I continue to cry, I feel stronger every day. As for now, my girls are calling me. This dancing queen has to get back on the floor.

The Great Pretenders

Grace Kuikman

During the summer of 1967, short, stout Gretchen Russo started a diet with her tall, thin best friend Martha "Martie" Mazita serving as coach and conscience. On the first day back at school, the girls sat together in the South Central Junior High lunch room. Gretchen pouted as Martie opened her brown lunch bag and checked each item, slid the melba toast, celery and slice of American cheese across the table toward Gretchen. She kept the Oreos.

"Leave me just one," Gretchen implored.

Martie, who ate constantly and never gained an ounce, moved the cookies farther out of Gretchen's reach. "Absolutely not."

"Why can't I have a high metabolism?" Gretchen sighed. She carefully folded the piece of cheese in half then half again, tore it along the folds and placed one piece each on the four pieces of melba toast.

Gretchen pulled the strings off a piece of celery and watched Pete Robertson walk up to the jukebox. He had really gotten cute over the summer, Gretchen thought. *Really* cute. Suddenly self-conscious about her weight, she put down the celery and rolled what was left of her lunch into the brown bag and pushed it away.

Pete leaned against the jukebox and scanned the menu of songs. He grinned, dropped a quarter in the slot and pushed the same buttons for all three plays. As Pete swaggered back to his seat, the record dropped into place.

"Wild thing—you make my heart sing..."

Table by table sandwiches were halted in mid-bite and chocolate milk stalled in mid-sip. Some of the boys started slapping the tabletop in time to the song's deliberate rhythm, and soon the entire room was slapping along. When the song immediately played again, a few of the kids started singing along. On the third play, everyone was singing at the top of their lungs.

"Wild thing, I think you move me."

The jukebox was stocked with 45s that the principal had deemed appropriate for pre-teens. Naïve love songs by The Beatles; The Beach Boys' surfing songs; that annoyingly hummable "Guantanamero." Who knows how the Troggs' hit *Wild Thing* got on there, but there it was: A-21.

Gretchen folded her arms over her still ample midriff and gazed at Pete. Arms raised and waving in time to the music, Pete was singing so loudly, Gretchen swore she could hear his voice.

A nice, conventional suburban school with nice, conventional students, most of the girls at South Central still wore dresses every day. Most of the boys had their hair cut short and neat. But a few of the kids had had traded in their Bermuda shorts and sun dresses for faded bell bottom jeans, tie-dye bandanas and fringed jackets. Already made suggestible by hormones and the scenes from the Viet Nam War their parents watched on the nightly news, these kids were ready—if not for revolution, for something.

The year before, Pete Robertson's oldest brother, Ted, had signed up to go to Viet Nam straight out of high school. For a while, it seemed like it would be OK, but then the family didn't hear from Ted for several weeks, and then a young man in a crisp Army uniform came to the Robertson's front door with a flag and sincere condolences from the appreciative people of the United States.

Pete's mother had been in a teary fog ever since. She neglected the housework and cooking, especially neglected Pete because he was alive and he wasn't Ted.

Pete made a point of being away from his house as much as possible. Over the summer, he put together a band with Chip Miller, Tony Valente and Paul Mullins. They called themselves the Great Pretenders and practiced almost every night in the Miller's garage. Kids started hanging out, listening to the music, occasionally lighting up a smoke or passing around a can of beer poured into a plastic pop glass. Long legged girls in hip-huggers and halter tops sat cross-legged on the concrete, staring at Pete from behind their wire-rim sunglasses. For Pete, that summer ended too soon.

When he dropped a quarter into the lunchroom jukebox on the second day of school, selecting A-21 for three spins, "Wild Thing" was locked in as the 8th grade anthem and Pete Robertson already knew that those kids were singing for him.

"Wild thing—you make my heart sing ... "

Watching Pete stride up to the jukebox was the highlight of Gretchen Russo's school days. "Wild thing, I think I love you ..." she would sing silently, a nervous thrill worming through her stomach.

"It must be true that your stomach shrinks when you eat less," she told Martie during the second week of school. "I'm never hungry anymore. I've lost six pounds."

"Good job," Martie said, picking over Gretchen's uneaten lunch for whatever looked good.

Gretchen was already watching when Pete rose from the table and strode to the jukebox. He raised his hands and the room quieted.

"I just want to let you guys know that my band, The Great Pretenders, will be playing at the sock hop tonight," he said. "I better see you all!"

The kids clapped and whistled. Pete grinned, dropped a quarter into the jukebox, and pushed A-21 three times.

The Great Pretenders set up their amps and microphones as members of the Student Council finished decorating. The lunchroom was steadily filling with kids. Gretchen arrived just after seven and caught sight of Martie across the room.

"Hey, Gretch," Martie said as her friend walked up. "The new top looks groovy."

Gretchen pulled at it self-consciously. Martie had convinced her to buy it, and it was shorter, lower cut and tighter than the tops she usually wore. "Do you really think so?" she said. "I'm not too fat?"

Martie's answer was lost in a screech of feedback as Pete Robertson leaned toward the microphone. Pete took a half step back, broke into that sensational grin, then tried again. "Ladies and gentlemen, introducing the new rock-and-roll sensation in their first appearance on the South Central Junior High stage—The Grrrrreat Pretenders!"

Pete held his guitar straight up in front of him and crashed his pick against the strings. Amps burst into sound. Just like the bands on "The Ed Sullivan Show", The Great Pretenders wore matching outfits: black turtlenecks, black pants, and black Beatle boots.

Their first song—"Secret Agent Man"—got everyone in the room clapping and singing along; a few brave girls even started dancing, though not with the boys. The music had a lot of rough spots, but to the sock hop crowd, it sounded great. Chaperones moved around the dance floor, but there were no groping couples to separate.

The band's second song, a slightly choppy rendition of The Association's "Cherish," had all the girls sighing. By the time the band got to "Mr. Tambourine Man," all the kids were up dancing. When they swung into their theme song, "The Great Pretender," the chaperones decided they could slip out for a smoke and a quick nip from the flask Mr. Peterson had stashed in the trunk of his Olds '98.

At nine o'clock, the lights came up in the gym. By all accounts, the first-ever South Central sock hop with a live band was a success. The principal announced that The Great Pretenders would be playing every week until further notice. The band started packing up their equipment, winding up thick black cords and carefully placing their shiny new guitars into shiny new guitar cases. Martie and Gretchen made their way toward the door. As they passed the stage, Gretchen blurted out, "You were WON-derful, Pete!"

Pete Robertson looked up, his flirty showman's smile still on his handsome face, and winked. "Why thanks, Gretchen. You made my night!"

Gretchen stopped and blinked. Martie pushed her toward the door. "C'mon, Gretch, my mom's waiting in the car."

All weekend, Gretchen played her 45 of The Platters singing "The Great Pretender" on the record player and Pete's words in her head. "You made my night. You made my night. You made my night." She closed her eyes and saw it again and again: that wink. But when she opened her eyes her bulky form looked back from her mirror. "That's what he sees," Gretchen groaned. "I'm still so fat!" She picked up the sandwich her mom made for her lunch and tossed it into the wastebasket. "No more sandwiches for me."

0

"The diet is working, Gretch," Martie said Monday as the girls walked into the lunchroom. "You're lookin' good!"

"I wish," Gretchen said. "I have so much to lose."

Gretchen nibbled on grapes while Martie consumed everything else Gretchen's mom packed into her lunch. Gretchen was skipping breakfast every morning and picking at dinner every night. After finishing her homework she often took out her Mom's sewing kit and stitched the seams of her dresses.

She lived for Friday nights, sighing over Pete through every song, then stopping by the stage on her way out, summoning the courage to say it again and again, "You were WON-derful, Pete," and to hear his well-rehearsed reply: "Thanks, Gretchen! You made my night!" She loved school lunch times. "Wild Thing—you make my heart sing…"

Pete's small attentions made Gretchen even more determined. As the weight melted away she bought skimpier clothes that she stashed in her purse at home then changed into at the gas station before heading to hang out with Martie.

"You're eating like a bird," her dad said at dinner one night. "You're going to waste away to nothing."

"Oh, Edward, shush," Gretchen's mom chided. "She's just growing up into a young lady, that's all; losing her baby fat. You keep doing whatever you're doing, Gretchen. One of these days you'll be as beautiful as your sister."

⸎

"We have a really great show lined up for you tonight," Pete announced.

It was the last sock hop before Christmas vacation. Earlier in the week the principal had removed "Wild Thing" from the lunchroom jukebox. The kids were busy with Christmas parties and performances, so they didn't complain much. But when they did, she said it was scratched and needed to be replaced. Actually, she thought South Central's 8th grade "wild things" had gotten out of control, playing that song over and over again, screaming out lyrics she suspected held some suggestive meaning. *Wild thing, I think you move me.*

The Great Pretenders opened the sock hop with a set of soft, danceable tunes. Gretchen arrived late. She left her house swimming in a bulky sweater and wool skirt, then snuck into the girls washroom to change into brand new skin-tight bell bottoms and a paisley halter top. "You're skinny!" Martie said when Gretchen stepped out of the bathroom at the gas station. "I mean it, you're actually *skinny*."

"Not yet," Gretchen said.

The girls walked into the gym. Gretchen found a spot that offered the perfect view of Pete on stage. Almost everyone was dancing, and the chaperones had little to do.

"Let's go," Mr. Peterson said as he took Mrs. Fletcher's elbow and escorted her out to his '98. Once the chaperones disappeared, Pete whispered into the microphone: "We've been practicing..."

He rammed out the first riff of The Rolling Stones' "Paint it Black." Students stood in surprised silence. This was not a song from the principal's "approved list." Without missing a beat, the band swung into "The House of the Rising Sun," then "Gloria" then "Louie, Louie." With each forbidden song, the kids got more pumped.

"This next song is for our biggest fans: Gretchen, Monica, Wendy . . . " As Pete continued listing the names of just about every girl in class, the band turned up their amps and broke into a deafening rendition of "Wild Thing." After a week of lunch time silence, the kids went berserk, screaming out the lyrics, pounding chairs on the floor, throwing paper cups of Hawaiian Punch that spilled in bloody red arcs onto the gym floor.

At the sound of her name moving over Pete's lips, Gretchen Russo fainted. Martie saw her go down, but thought it was a joke. When Gretchen didn't get back up, Martie started to panic. "Get Mr. Peterson and Mrs. Fletcher!"

From somewhere deep in her starving brain, Gretchen recognized the voices of her classmates, curiously soft and sonorous, not anything like the tuneless screamy singing she was used to hearing in the lunchroom. "Wild thing—I think I love you...."

While Mrs. Fletcher looked up Gretchen's telephone number to call her parents, Mr. Peterson drove the unconscious girl to the emergency room. They started an IV. "This girl is starving," she heard someone yell. "Didn't anyone notice this?" From a dreamy place that she would frequently visit over many years she'd spend starving herself, the voice inside Gretchen's head softly sang, drowning out the sounds of the doctors and nurses all around her. "Wild thing—you make my heart sing..." Boys are addictions that come and go. Other addictions last a lifetime.

The Great Pretenders broke up just after Christmas. In winter it was too cold to practice in the Miller's garage and no one wanted the band playing in their basement. Gretchen was still in the hospital when it happened; Martie could hardly wait for visiting hours so she could tell her best friend the news. Pete put his guitar in the closet, next to a box filled with his brother Ted's perfect report cards and baseball trophies.

The South Central principal never did get a new copy of "Wild Thing" for the jukebox. But it didn't matter. By the time everyone got back to school in January, they were ready for a new song.

Symphony #10

Robert Lawrence

Last night,
I resuscitated Beethoven.
(DNA from his lead-tainted hair?
Never mind how).
I seated him comfortably
on my living room couch,
served him black coffee
and a slice of lemon strudel.
I spoke to him in German
(translated for your ease):
"You've gotta hear this."

I played a recording
of the first movement
of his tenth symphony
(orchestrated by someone else),
then composers posthumous
to Ludwig, their harmonies moving
with the inevitability of gravity
towards jarring dissonance,
paralleling the transition in art
from *Liberty Leads the People*
to the abstract expressionist colorswirl
hanging on my wall.

I thought he'd spurn the moderns
with wrath, as on his deathbed
when he sat up and shook his fist
at the thundering heavens. Instead
he motioned for more coffee and said,
"My God, I can hear again!
Everything is so beautiful,
even your strange accent."

Stream of Consciousness

Diane L. Lewis

Fingers. Press. Hot. Against
skin that hasn't seen August sunlight
or felt cool October breezes
for a while

Fingers. Play. Black. Keys
on instruments made for
loving in E sharp

Wild. Strong. Hands. Heavy
on the hips
immobilize thighs til
heat from veined black keys
melts "Kimball" clean off
burnished pieces lie about
like panties on bedroom floors

Finger. Prints. Lifted. From crime scenes--
heart stolen, music arrested while
high on Coltrane-blow
drunk on cool blues tones
intoxicated on Thelonious Monk. . . you

Ice. Cold. Miles. Cool
the black keys down
until syncopation
stirs the pot and the rhythm
of copulation resumes.
the touch of a thousand hammers
vibrate uncontrollably

Weary. Hands. Find. Places. Resting
while the pulse of love begins afresh

I. Am. Falling. In. Love. With. You.

Ted Nugent Needn't Be Explained

Mardi Jo Link

We are on our way to soccer practice when my fifteen-year-old son plugs his green iPod into the car stereo, cutting off National Public Radio like a hip-hop record scratch. But not before I learn this breaking news: Ted Nugent, the musical hero of my youth, the man who irritated and confused my parents in much the same way that rap music irritates and confuses me, has some explaining to do. According to NPR, the musician whose loincloth and loin-centered lyrics threated my girlhood in the 1970s, has expanded his range. Today, Ted threatens Homeland Security.

Here are the facts the radio reporter delivered, right before my son cut her off: Several agents from President Obama's Secret Service detail recently called on Ted Nugent at his ranch in Texas. At a gun conference, Ted had expressed some odd notions regarding Obama's suitability to lead the free world, and the agents were just following up. Their arrival began as an official visit, but turned into a barbecue. Standard firearm protocol was not—and NPR was quite clear on this—observed.

Instead, the secret service traipsed out back with the Motor City Madman, into the scrub and hardpack of Ted's vast acreage, to do a little target shooting. Then gleefully handed over their service weapons to Ted, which he used to go Double Live Gonzo.

But I scarcely have a moment to process this news before my son intervenes with his iPod, makes his musical selection, and then rhythmic explosions burst from my car's speakers.

"Jay-Z is just so *great*," my son says.

These two consonants—J and Z—vaguely register in my middle-aging brain as a musician. A rapper whom I think I remember being interviewed on MSNBC. Then the full capabilities of aftermarket automotive subwoofers are on display in the tight confines of my new SUV. There's a bottle of Gatorade on my son's lap and the lime-green liquid pulses.

"Why's he so great?" I ask. I mean, I yell. Straining. On. Each. Word.

"He's just so *creative*," my son yells back. But he yells it cool.

The awe in his voice makes me think of Ted, who was my musical hero when I was a teenager. Not the Texas Ted of today, but the Michigan Ted of 1979. The Ted who wrote and played a good portion of the rock and roll soundtrack to my sneaky youth. By day, I was on the swim team and the honor roll. After school, I knew which liquor stores sold beer to sixteen-year-old girls and how to make a bong out of an apple.

I look over at my son and marvel at his goodness. So far, he exhibits none of his mother's youthful rebellion. By day, he plays soccer and is on the honor roll. After school, he drinks Gatorade and can solve a Rubik's Cube in 45 seconds. This characterization is not just wishful thinking. He and I spend so much time together, either at soccer tournaments or at home, where all his friends like to hang out, that he simply doesn't have time to get into trouble. Soon, though, he'll turn sixteen. A driver's license can change everything. It did for me. Will Jay-Z be the soundtrack to his misbehavior? I focus on the man my son idolizes and make a point to listen to his lyrics. The ones my son says are creative.

Give some thought to your musical heroes, I want to advise him. Please. Learn from your mother. Because if what I'm feeling right now about Ted is any indication, then later—OK, perhaps much later— your choice of heroes today could precipitate an existential quandary tomorrow.

I open my mouth to begin this conversation, but see my son's uncomplicated teenage face in repose and say nothing. His eyes are closed and he is deep into his music. I know that feeling. And remembering, it takes me back.

It was the summer of 1979 in Bay City, the thumb pit of Michigan. I was a sullen high school junior, just a year older than my son is now, and stuck in the suburbs with a Farah Fawcett haircut and a taste for arena rock. The Sony Walkman, my generation's answer to the iPod, wasn't even invented yet. The way to experience music was live, in person, and with 20,000 other fans, not piped privately into your ears, or into your mother's car stereo, by a tiny machine.

Besides soccer, music is everything to my son. He uses it to survive the monotonous bus ride to school, to make homework less lame, even to define himself to himself. When he listens to Jay-Z, he is his own personal version of Jay-Z.

I know that because, let me tell you dude, I took my music serious, too. When I was a teenager and listened to *Free For All*, I became my own personal version of Terrible Ted. In July of 1979, I loaded my best girlfriends into my parent's old Oldsmobile a half dozen times. The glove box was so big, it could hold two six packs. We roadtripped it to Flint, Saginaw, and Detroit, and pressed up to the stage where Foghat, Peter Frampton, Blue Oyster Cult, Bob Seeger, Van Halen, and Nazareth held sway.

All we needed was a little more gas money and we'd make it to Ted, Ozzie, and Led before the start of senior year. Then later that summer, a local DJ delivered some terrific news via my boombox: My girlfriends and I wouldn't have to drive very far to see Ted after all, because he was coming to us. He'd be headlining an outdoor concert right there in Bay City! "Summer Celebration '79," the disc jockey said, would rock our town in just a couple of weeks.

I called my girlfriends with the news.

"It's zee Wango," I told them, quoting Ted, "and zee Tango."

Back then, I knew nothing about Ted's gun stance or his politics. I didn't know decades into the future he would teach the model/actress/porn star Tia Tequila, a guest on his reality show, how to build an outhouse. I didn't know he'd poach a bear in Alaska or name his 2010 tour, "Trample the Weak, Hurdle the Dead." I didn't know he'd threaten a U.S. President whom I wholeheartedly voted for, twice. And I certainly didn't know he'd author a bestselling cookbook that would include a recipe for Squirrel Casserole.

At seventeen, I only knew that he of the loincloth, of the Jesus hair, and the nature-loving ballad, "Great White Buffalo," would be in my hometown. I only knew that the Nuge would be playing live, just across the river from my house, right on the football field of a rival high school.

I only knew that I was going.

⸱ 🐾 ⸱

My son and I arrive at the Keystone Soccer Complex and he busts a couple core dance moves from the passenger seat before unplugging his iPod. While he sways I try to imagine Jay-Z in thirty years. I don't know a thing about his politics and my son probably doesn't either. How important are the worldviews of our musical heroes when they have nothing to do with the music they play? Maybe it depends on how old you are, and whether or not you are a parent. Not so important when you're a teenager; more important when you're that teenager's mother.

Perhaps Jay-Z won't trample anything in the next three decades. Perhaps in thirty years my son will even still admire him. All I still admire about Ted is what lured me to him in the first place. His music.

I try to imagine the Jay-Z of today playing a concert for high school kids here in town at our local football stadium, and it seems impossible. He is too famous, too rich, too distant. Despite the drinking and drugs and secrecy that informed my adolescence, it still seems more difficult to be a teenager today than it was in 1979. Everything is dangerous. Cars, school, even music. None of the hair bands I followed shot each other. Random violence and imagined slights make it impossible for any famous musician to show up in a small town like ours, plug in, and rock out. Or, rap out, as the case may be.

My son is safe with me, yet lives in a world that is not. In a world where musicians threaten the president and the agents who are supposed to protect him shirk their duty. Back in the summer of 1979, my biggest problem was getting a ticket for Ted's sold-out summer concert.

— 🐾 —

That day, it stormed. The football field was a swamp and the warm-up band only played for half an hour before they left the stage, afraid of being electrocuted by their own equipment. The warm-up band was The Babys, a name my friends and I laughed at after booing their chicken-shit exit. As they flipped off the crowd, we joined with the other 22,000 muddy, shivering and ecstatic fans screaming, "Ted! Ted! Ted!"

And then, there he was.

A madman with a guitar. Naked except for a loincloth and hair longer than mine, swinging from a twenty-foot-long rope and landing barefoot on top of an amplifier as big as a boulder. He shredded the first chords of "Stormtroopin" just as thunder annihilated the drum solo and lightening cracked the sky in half.

"Get ready!" my hero wailed, "Stormtroopers comin'!"

Ted played for more than two hours without a break. Then he played three encores. In the rain, in the thunder, in the lightening and barefoot, he played. He was bigger than The Babys, bigger than Bay City, bigger even than the natural laws of electricity and I was in awe.

— 🐾 —

The car door closes, my son grins and waves, and I watch him jog away, down the hill toward the soccer field. The car is quiet again, no

Jay-Z, no Motor City Madman. I turn NPR back on and hear the newsman say that you just can't threaten the President, even if you know how to shoot the Secret Service's guns. *Especially* if you know how to shoot the Secret Service's guns.

Ted's comment about President Obama has shocked even hard-core fans of his music like me. The announcer says that despite that friendly barbeque, and despite his popularity in the 1970's, he will still have to answer some hard questions. I listen to NPR in the coming days, awaiting his response. He eventually gives one.

"Metaphors," Ted says, "needn't be explained to educated people."

Man, that's weak. I don't know what I expected him to say, but it wasn't that. And yet, I can still hear the sound of his guitar. Over the thunder, over the lightening, through all the years and even above his deranged politics, I can still hear it.

I can't explain it, but I can hear it.

One of his hit songs, "Free For All," which is a song about letting loose, but also about loyalty, pops into my head. Then the next week unfolds like every other week and on a sunny afternoon I'm back at the soccer field to pick up my son. He slides into the car, sweaty and grinning. I hand him his iPod and brace myself for the kick from the speakers.

"Listen," the rapper with two consonants for a name chants, "Momma *loved* me."

I tune out Jay-Z's other consonants, the ones I disapprove of, the Fs and the Ns, and try to focus on the creativity my son hears. And I try to remember, too, what he talked about when MSNBC interviewed him. It's a news show. What about Jay-Z was news? Was he involved in a shooting?

It takes me a few minutes, but then I recall why MSNBC invited the rapper to appear on their show. He pledged a lot of money—$1 million maybe—to continue rebuilding New Orleans after Katrina, dedicated one of his world tours to addressing the global water shortage, and started a scholarship fund for non-traditional students. After all his rap riches, Jay-Z didn't want to talk about gun rights and violence, he wanted to talk about philanthropy.

Mullet-head that I am, I yell this realization to my son.

"I know, right?" he yells back. Eyes closed. Still cool.

I reach for the volume and turn it up. Just a little. Our musical heroes, my son and I wordlessly agree, really needn't be explained.

.
.
.

100

.
.
.

Music on My Mind

Margaret Lisle

Last year I dreamt of Mayor Richard J. Daley, former and deceased mayor of Chicago, Illinois.

Big as life he was. In Technicolor! We were dancing, which right there validates it could only have been a dream. I can't imagine Richard J. dancing—ever. Well, maybe on his wedding day when tradition obliged him. It was a mystery to me why he appeared in one of my dreams and it gnawed at me to distraction. My connection to him during this lifetime was slim and secondhand. My first husband's father was one of his pals and a groomsman at his wedding to Sis. I did attend his daughter Carol's wedding and in later years came to have a nodding acquaintance with his sons, mostly because of my job as secretary to another prominent politician. I deeply admired the man and was one of the hundreds of mourners who stood in long lines to pay their respects at his funeral.

I tried unsuccessfully to identify the song we were dancing to in my dream because I sensed it was somehow important, but I could only remember a few bars: the beginning refrain and parts of the bridge. The ending eluded me. I kept going over it in my head, sometimes out loud, but it wasn't reminiscent of any song I had ever heard before. It was a happy song, though Richard J. wasn't smiling. His face was sober and all concentration, perhaps on getting the beat of the music right. He looked like a man who was doing something against his better judgment. I didn't have time to wonder why we were dancing together as the dream was over that fast and I awoke.

The dream came back every night for a week. It was always the same: Richard J. and I were dancing to a happy song, but he wasn't smiling and looked as though he didn't want to be there. Just as I became aware of the music, the dream ended. It sounded a lot like a country-western tune, a style close to my heart, but one I would never associate with Richard J. Listening to music would probably have been very low on his list of priorities. He had little time to enjoy music for its own sake; he was too busy listening to the beat of his City, which he loved passionately.

I like listening to music. All kinds, except for Rap, which I don't consider music. I've even tried my hand at composing. I wrote some music to accompany the lyrics of the Alcoholic Anonymous "Serenity" prayer; but never tried to get it published. I thought perhaps that might be the message in my dream-clip: *Get your music out there. Finish what you started.*

I read somewhere how Paul McCartney heard the music to his song, "Yesterday," in a dream and figured it out on a piano when he awoke. I also read that music in dreams represents harmony and the infinite potential of creative life. Was the Universe nudging me? Was I being given information that my conscious self didn't understand but my heart did? I knew this much: I'd never heard the song before. Was the message the song itself, I wondered? Perhaps Richard J. was bringing me a chance, an opportunity to take the refrain, add some lyrics and make it mine. Perhaps his presence represented the fame that would come with a hit tune.

Operating on this theory, I started to listen to the song in my head with a different point of view. It was lovely, melodic, feel-good music. Lyrics began to form, gushing from me like automatic writing, as if the words had been there all the time, just waiting for me to release them. There was no hesitation on my part, the words and music connected without a doubt of their creation. Richard J. had brought me a gift from the Other Side, a melody I could mold. I felt an urgency to finish the song as soon as possible. Therein lay the rub. There was a beginning and a middle, but no ending. I was stuck! Nothing came to me. I asked the Universe for help. I prayed to Richard J., whom I now considered my muse. No response. I went to bed praying the dream would return, bringing an ending. For the first time in eight nights there were no dreams at all.

I kept trying on my own and came close, but no cigar. I finally gave up and put away what I had written. That night I dreamed I was dancing with Richard J. again but to a different tune. This time he was smiling, the song was upbeat and seemed vaguely familiar. He looked happy to be with me. We were almost cutting a rug. The song had a beginning, a middle, and an ending. When the music was over, he turned to face me, took hold of my hands, looked me in the eyes and said: "Believe." I awoke immediately, feeling refreshed and excited, ready to try again.

After much angst and tearing out of hair I did finish the song, which I called "Believe." It became a hit single and is still selling after ten months. I've been told the song is inspirational and will probably become a classic. Richard J., my song-and-dance man, has not returned with any more heavenly music, but he's not far from my thoughts and prayers. If he does choose to visit again, I hope he brings me a waltz. I think this technological world filled with loud, screaming-meemie music really needs a waltz, don't you?

Love Me Tender in Midlife

Ellaraine Lockie

I was fourteen
and a Future Homemaker of America
when Elvis swiveled
his *Let's Play House* inhibitions
in moves that made Montana girls blush
from Miles City to Big Sandy

Brandishing a guitar instead of a gun
and giving new meaning to movement
his fence-free brand of bawdy
disfigured the flesh of milk-fed morality
indelible marks on all
but the most proprietary complexions

Mine flashing Pat Boone flawless
above goodie two shoes
instead of *Blue Suede Shoes*
straitlaced in Luther League straps
and protected by a preacher
who condemned Elvis as *Devil in Disguise*
his songs subjects of Sunday sermons

So he served a forty-year sentence
during my matrimonial
and maternal hard labor
before exonerating himself postmortem
far from the convent of Montana convention
in my California midlife conversion

Where my unblemished body
has been tattooed by release
indelible marks that appoint permission
to move in *Any Way You Want It*
when *One Night With You*
replaces up-tight with you
and the rhythm of new religion
resonates Elvis animation
through the limbs of a liberated woman

The Plight of the Tuba

Terry Loncaric

Big head,
strange, curvy neck,
the poor, sad, lonely tuba
always stuck in the back row,
until he releases
a gigantic belch,
a marshmallow swirl
of sweet, puffing sounds.
He laughs and grunts
while he repeats his refrain.
The clouds rumble,
the kids smile,
the other instruments
take notice of the
big kid in the back row.

Jazz Morning Drive

Terry Loncaric

Jazz perks, sizzles,
jangly, juicy music
sweeps smoggy air,
shimmers sunlight,
sax wails, moans,
cymbals whisper,
light kisses,
bass thumps,
slow seduction,
breathless joy ride,
unexpected riffs,
flood of emotions,
slither, hiss, sputter,
snake charmer, jazz cats
drench the sleepy day,
exclamation marks of joy.

⋮

106

⋮

No Place like Home

Barb LoPresti

The nurse pushed the wheelchair in front of the mirror and tucked a blanket around his weakened legs before leaving the room. He stared at his reflection, then glanced at the image of his old friend, the cowardly lion, standing hunchbacked beside him.

"Look at us," said the tin man, his voice like the sound of a rusted hinge. "It's my fault." He reached up and with his knotted fingers, he traced his sunken cheeks, covered in ashen skin. A sorrowful look clouded his steel-blue eyes. "When I asked you to leave Oz and follow me somewhere over the rainbow, I didn't know we would change and become human."

The lion laid a large, paw-like hand on the tin man's frail shoulder, "Ah, my friend," the lion purred, "we were changed the moment she came into in our lives." A sparkle lit up the lion's large, brown eyes as he raised his bushy eyebrows and slowly shook his head in a gesture that said he had no regrets. "It was her belief in me that gave me the courage to come here with you," he said, staring down at the tin man. As the lion continued, a smile crossed his face, lifting his saggy jowls. "The years I've spent here in Kansas have given me the opportunity to fulfill my dreams, becoming Mayor, king of the city."

The tin man looked out beyond his reflection and his thoughts turned to their companion made out of straw, who'd many years ago turned down his invitation to join him and the lion on his heart-felt quest to locate the girl. A few weeks back, the tin man had suffered a heart attack, and he remembered how the wizard had come to visit him here in the hospital. The wizard had brought along his crystal ball and after a few waves of his wizened hands over the magical round sphere, the scarecrow's image had appeared. A great sadness had wrenched the tin man's stomach as he watched his youthful scarecrow friend wiling away the hours suspended on a pole in the middle of a cornfield, scaring the crows, his brilliant mind still busy hatching thoughts of becoming the scholar of Oz. His focus returned to the reflection of his metallic self and his . The tin man mused at the appearance of his friend's portly frame and balding head with the remaining strands of his long hair tied in a ponytail at the nape of his thick neck. Yet he still beamed with life.

The nurse's shoe's squeaked against the polished floors as she walked into the room. The lion turned around. Glancing at her name badge, he extended his hand and in a deep, welcoming voice he said, "Hello, Linda, it's nice to see someone in such good spirits taking care of my good friend. In his stay in the hospital's west wing, he had such a wicked witch of a nurse."

The grin on Linda's face broadened as she gestured a quick nod of greeting and shook the lion's hand. "Good afternoon, Mayor Lionel," she said, a hint of a southern drawl in her voice. Then she steered the tin man's wheelchair toward the bed. The joints in his artificial knees creaked as she helped him up. "Okay Mr. Tinmin, it's time to get you dressed and ready to go home."

A set of heels clicked down the hallway and stopped in the entrance of the tin man's room. He glanced at the doorway and for him a symphony of love songs filled the air. Even after all these years, the sight of his wife made his heart twitter like a happy little bluebird. A blush colored his cheeks as he threw a sideways glance at his old pal across the room.

The lion stepped forward. "Hello, Dorothy," he said, lowering his gaze while he bowed his head.

Dorothy stood in the threshold, her petite, slightly stooped frame in a light-blue gingham dress, her gray hair styled in a single French braid that hung midway down her back, a box of munchkin donuts in her hand. She glanced between the two aging men. A smile crossed her face, deepening the creases etched in the skin around her sparkling brown eyes and in a musical tone, she said, "There really is no place like home."

Blossoming

Tracey Ludvik

I am a green magnolia bud
a lotus whose patient petals
are wrapped tightly inside
my hard cone shield
sitting upright upon green, well-polished leaves
showered in streams of rain and sun
standing up to the wind
waiting...

for the perfect breath of air
to crack open my sheath
liberate my silken white petals to
unfold one by one
a sacred flower reflecting
perfumed sunlight back into the sky
that can be heard if you listen

The Art of Asking

Shahé Mankerian

The old man adjusts
his bowtie and struts out
of the fake ballroom fog
in a white polyester suit.

He tags the lone Angeleno
with a flip of his sweaty
handkerchief. Her hips,
glued to the stool,

can't avoid the aging rooster.
He plants his cigar
in her ashtray, clears
the bangs from her eyes,

and points with his cane
toward the dimming spotlight.
She lifts her skirt above
her thighs and follows him.

Her heels scrape the tile
as she spins. Her spine feels
like saxophone keys beneath
his fingers. The jitter

of maracas fade; the music
shifts from yambú to guaguancó.
She wants to check her mascara
and the lines of her stocking

in the crowded bathroom.
He leads her to the bar,
kisses her hand and offers
the red carnation form his lapel.

Here on the Edge of Desert

Terry Martin

I'd like to send you a morning like this.
Golden sun on stubbled fields,
hills tawny as a lion's flank.
Sage and stillness, sky and quiet.

I'd like to give you this
glimpse of clear blue
where two hawks circle,
riding their thermals.

Offer you fists of flowers,
blooming in our desert garden:
hollyhocks, star lilies,
poppies and roses

scents carried on air
calling you home,
to things you left
but failed to get away from.

I'd like to invite you
to pluck ripe fruit
from our backyard tree,
feast on peach after peach.

When you hear these finches sing
their songs that have to be sung,
feel them filling your lungs,
you'll know the gold is here.

Kill-Zone Requiem

Dennis Maulsby

We wade through jungle shadows. Sweat drips
off our tiger-striped fatigues to wet red Asian soil.
Boots scuff, release fermented biting odors.
Butterflies blink wing eyes, shimmy dragon tails.

Insects in droning click-bodied clouds flutter,
nip, creep. Saw-toothed leaves and vine thorns
scarify our necks and arms. The clack of hornbills,

the chortle of long-tail macaques set the tempo.
The bass drum beat of mortars firing slaps
our cheeks. Explosions shake triple canopy trees

their creaking limbs a pizzicato of violin and cello.
Bodies crazy-dance to the brass cymbal screech
of slicing shrapnel. We hear the tremolo drumstick

smack of jacketed bullets pierce canvas, cloth,
flesh. The splintered oboe thunk-grunt of metal
embedding in wood creates jittering chords.

Smoke-curdled air quivers with the clarinet warble
of blunt-nosed ricochets. We dying give up
a final fugue of voices. Jumbled echoes fade,
weep off elephant grass, strangling fig, twisted lianas.

Angels in the Architecture

Kathleen McElligott

As a child I believed everything that the nuns at Our Lady of Perpetual Despondence told us. I was a pudgy kindergartener in my navy blue uniform with bolero jacket and A-line skirt, ready to drink the Kool-Aid.

My first opportunity was when Sister told the class, five-year-olds separated from their mothers for the first time, how the world was going to end—fire and brimstone and dead people rising from their graves. It was a done deal. The only remedy was to be a good Catholic—a brilliant mind-game.

I was terrified, my insides knotted with fear. In a daze I wandered around the playground. It didn't seem to faze the other kids, who ran and played Red Rover like any other day. Maybe they had an inner filter that told them not to take this stuff too seriously.

At dismissal I ran home to my safe zone. If the world was going to end I wanted to be with Mom and Dad and my cat, Fluffy. I stared at my mother while she made dinner. Did she know about this and not tell me? What other stuff was she keeping from me? How does a five-year-old express betrayal and fear? Not well. I kept it all inside.

First grade was better; no horrifying biblical revelations. I was as squirrely as my fellow baby-boomers, fifty to a class. No wonder the nuns used psychological warfare to keep us in line. School was boring. I excelled at staring out the window during arithmetic and dropped my pencil repeatedly so I could crawl under the table to pick it up. Eventually, I'd raise my hand and ask a question. *See, I'm paying attention.*

This behavior didn't go unnoticed. Mom got home from parent-teacher conference and sat me down at the kitchen table. "Sister says you ask random questions, completely off-topic." Her cold stare said it all: *Stop asking weird questions and try to fit in.*

Second grade was promising. The entire year was spent preparing for first Communion. Instead of doom and gloom, the topic switched to angels. This was a bandwagon I could climb aboard. Angels were magical—from the everyday Guardian variety to the upper echelon, the Archangels. Who knew that Lucifer was once the most beautiful and brightest of all until he got too big for his britches? I was all in, and for a time stopped daydreaming and dropping things.

It was a warm and humid Saturday. Spring thunderstorms boomed and flashed all day. I stood by the screen door watching as the last storm clouds skittered away. A rainbow appeared over the rooftops, hazy at first, then transforming into a vibrant arch of color. As it intensified, a heavenly chorus rose, filling the universe with music unlike any I had ever heard. It had no words, only a haunting melody that crescendoed and drifted heavenward. I had no doubt, none whatsoever, that the angels were singing. I was eager to believe and turned to my mother, hoping she'd heard it, too.

"Do you hear them?" I asked.

"Hear what?" she replied.

"The angels." *Of course, the angels. Why couldn't she hear them?*

I stood silently and listened, until the rainbow and the joyful choir faded away. It lasted about a minute and when it was over a peaceful feeling washed over me.

The innocence of a child is a precious gift. I was eager to believe that angels sing, and for me, they did. Like the silver sleigh bell in the *Polar Express*, the world is full of miracles for those whose hearts are open to wonder. Choose to believe in miracles.

At Seventeen

Karla Linn Merrifield

Who was that cute boy,
brother as clean-cut teen,
with a folk guitar,
beardless chin to the mic
in the Franklin gym?
Who was my brother then, senior year,
with Gene in the middle, full-throated,
and Pete, nonchalant on his banjo?
Were they doing *Tom Dooley* or *All My Trials*?
Something Kingston Trio, something
earliest Dylan, a PP&M number?

The photograph, 1964 vintage,
a high school Kodak moment,
depicts my brother emerging
from the robin's egg of innocence:
pre-Vietnam, pre-wine, pre-
long life of broken women.
The composition is such
there's no telling the truth,
but I like to believe
his audience danced, classmates
sang along that December night
for Jimmy's sake.

Following His Conducting Debut, ASIMO the Robot Complains of Sharing the Venue with Yo-Yo Ma

Carolyn Moore

French Horn brayed I lack the eyes
brass requires to drive it harder.
Cheeky tooter! Dare he preach
"drive" to *me*, whose belt boasts "Honda"?
(He's not fit to honk our cars!)

As for Ma, he's spread too thin:
Bach to Sting? And waltz to tango?
Schumann to McFerrin's scat?
How unlike my creed at Honda!
(One Thing Only: Do it Right.)

I could wheel him back on track,
steer him as his strict conductor.
Metronome's the best baton,
keeps things clipped in tidy measure.
(No improvisation gaffes.)

Dizzying, Ma's Silk Road quest!
Bringing back that music clutter—
gimcrack flutes and gewgaw strings.
No consumer wants such challenge
(wrenched from strange and foreign dreams).

Call this envy? Not a whit!
Ma's vast chaos cannot tempt me,
cannot coax me from my order.
How I'd miss my cozy safety
(life in snug parentheses).

Goose Music

Lylanne Musselman

In the Botanical Gardens, a man
plays the tin sculpture like a drum,
a young girl accompanies on flute –
sweet music fills the summer air.

A concert of geese, not satisfied to sit
as audience, horn their way
center stage, remind these humans
who trumpets symphonies in this park.

Rondo – Burleske

From Mahler's 9th Symphony, third movement

Marjorie Ryerson

Lusty winds, wanton and selfish,
recklessly flatten the pines
on the ridge. Grizzlies wail
in alarm. Meadows of wheat
fold as lightning
breaches the fertile soil.
The sky twists green.

Wake up. Watch out.
Disoriented deer and gray wolves
collide. Hedgehogs and lizards sprint
for shelters they cannot find.
Parrots scream. Vultures abandon
their bright meals.
Turn round quickly.
Time is under arrest.

Small voices whimper
and are drowned out.
Is anyone left who trusts solitude?
Can hearts still meld?
Who is listening?

Now, as opaque mist
settles on everything,
grace notes of light
comb the mist, like small breaths.
Trees emit final coughs
and settle back into wet ground,
their identities forgotten.
The mist curdles.
The light evaporates.

Jazz Mass for Kerouac's Navy

Lynn Veach Sadler

Jack Kerouac could have
gone down
on the *Dorchester* that day.

His friend, the black cook,
Old Glory, did die
on the *Dorchester* that day.

Kerouac deemed his "dead brother"
a saint, heard him
speak from Heaven before that day.

Kerouac had a habit
of scat-singing
with Gregorian chants—Jazz Mass.

Kerouac later left the Navy
for "angel tendencies,"
roamed the earth.

$\vdots$

120

$\vdots$

Early Morning Concerto at Beemer's Pond

Susanna Schuerman

The curtain rises to unveil a barren tree quivering in the wind, a rich hint of a cold, crisp day. I throw the blankets over my head and try to ignore the excited chatter of my photographer-husband, "Get up. We have to get there before the birds fly out."

Hmmm. Bill didn't get the memo that this is a vacation day – meant for sleeping in, drinking hot tea in my jammies or reading a mystery while wrapped in Grandma's handmade quilt' in other words, hibernating. There's no use arguing. We're heading out – and soon.

We are traveling to Beemer's Pond to photograph trumpeter swans. The hour and a half drive is sprinkled with talk of Iowa's autumn landscape. Amber waves of grain have turned to brown rows of stubble this November day. We have not yet received a blanket of snow to cover the monochrome palette. We spot a Red-Tailed hawk perched on a fence post, but very few creatures, feathered or human, stir on this frigid morning.

A curve in the gravel road brightens my face and transforms the drab landscape. I spot an-ice covered pond surging with life, the reward for our early morning journey. Hundreds of trumpeter swans, Canadian geese and mallards have claimed Beemer's Pond. Before I can pull on my sweatshirt, heavy coat, boots, ear muffs and scarf, Bill is already heading for the icy water. He is covered from head to foot in winter gear—only his hazel eyes visible as he peers through a slit in his face mask—his bare fingers positioned to snap the illusive perfect shot.

Swans, geese and mallards call to each other, creating a cacophony of sound. The bold, brassy blare of trumpeters directs the high-pitched honking of geese and the nasal quacking of hundreds of mallards. The swans' heads bob in rhythm to an unknown tune. Their graceful movement reminds me of a musician pressing the valves on a French horn.

The performance holds me spellbound. I'm an intruder on a feral orchestra warming up for their morning sonata. The raucous score brims with riotous calls, and the gallantry of out-stretched wings rivals any Vegas stage show.

Vigorously led by the trumpet of the swans, the sonata ebbs and flows until the band of feathered musicians stun their audience with sudden flight. The beat of hundreds of wings stills my breath. Bill's camera is clicking.

"Encore," I whisper.

Those Fool Birds

Art Schwartz

That bird who leaps into the sky
from the highest branch of my willow tree,
and find a perfect upward draft,
and sings those stupid songs of joy,
that bird's a fool to think he's happy

Looking for tall trees and perfect weather,
jumping off a thousand times, he never learns
it's not the way to once and for all possess
the thing he's jumping for, the fool forever
lusting after meaningless, clear roads above.

But I remember once, I saw this still,
and silent bird swaying on a sprig of elm
awhile without any urge, and then cry out
in such a way, as if he knew his song was sad,
when even he was forced to leap into the sky.

Melody

Don Segal

Your voice is like a melody;
a cheerful robin's song
that percolates the early hours
in darkness before dawn.

Not raucous ranting crowing caws
right in the bright of day
nor never ending sparrow chats
with nothing ever said.

Through air and through wire
by dark and metallic ways
your voice springs out as if alive
and sings to me and says,

How wonderful it is to talk.
How spectacular is the day!

Eat When Hungry, Sleep When Tired

a Zen saying

Marian Kaplun Shapiro

and then there is Chopin, meandering
from five impossible flats to four sharps
as if each measure were a casual ripple
in a spring stream of melting centuries.
What are we to make of him? *Nocturnes*
unnecessary as diamond necklaces,
fantasies frivolous as sequined
ballgowns. His *preludes* sing us into the land
of sadnesses deeper than the deepest
snowdrifts. His *valses* whirl us into that
last dance of the evening. They hold
us to each other. They show us the fire-
fly, the precious light before lightsout.
They teach us about breathing. When hungry,
eat. When tired, sleep.

Prairie Song

Julianza Shavin

In the treeless fields,
tumbleweeds—
round brown skeletons—
rip across the road
faster than cats or rabbits.
We don't hit them.

They flash like skinned
umbrellas
across the pavement
dividing parched plains.
Desolation fills us.

Skeletal remains
of sheep, cow, elk
fascinate the child,
who covets them, collects them,
brings some home
to show off.

On the prairie,
the wind blows through them
all night, all day
making of the bones
wind instruments,
making of mortality
a music.

⋮

126

⋮

Life's Glissando

Grazina Smith

When I was young, one of my jobs was to peel the potatoes and then pass them to Rachel so she could grate them for latkes. I kept my kitchen tasks a secret from my friends. At that time, boys just didn't do that kind of work. Even when I was in a hurry, I tried to keep the paring knife from slicing deep under the skin. I knew either mamah or Rachel would check the peels and judge their thickness, scolding me if they weren't thin enough. Rachel liked to correct me all day, about everything. She was taller than Mamah with dark hair that curled around her face and hung down her back, thick and tangled like a horse's mane. Rachel thought she was grown up because she'd turned 15 and was to start a job in the men's shirt factory. I sure didn't want to be grown up in four years.

The mound of peels almost covered the front page of the *Forward*, but I could still see the headline, "Roosevelt—Labor's Choice" and, underneath it, the drawing of a man with his hand on FDR's shoulder, like they were buddies or something. I noticed the drawing because the man looked like my Uncle Avrom, with an open-necked work shirt, a flat cap on his head and the hint of a smile on his broad face. Uncle Avrom was tateh's brother and had come from Omaha to live with us about two months ago. He took over my bed in the kitchen and mamah moved a cot to a corner of the parlor for me. Now, there were six of us in a two-bedroom apartment. I was the youngest and had no say about where I slept. Mamah and tateh had one bedroom and Rachel shared the other small room with grandma and, according to Rachel, our bubbe snored like a buzz saw.

Every day, Uncle Avrom lugged a heavy suitcase from door to door selling scarves, sweaters, shoelaces, washcloths, perfumed soaps, hairpins, combs, even ladies' garters. I tried to lift that suitcase once and it must have weighed a hundred pounds. Uncle Avrom laughed.

"Nu, you grow a little muscle and you can help me carry it all day." I hoped not. Every night, after dinner, Uncle Avrom rolled up his trousers and soaked his feet in a bucket of hot water, sighing about how much they hurt. He and tateh would sit at the table arguing politics while mamah washed the dishes and then did the mending. To look at them, the two brothers were not at all alike. Uncle Avrom was round and jolly with a halo of copper-colored hair that gleamed in the sunlight. A thick mustache decorated his face and he teased that it was a scrub brush he'd glued under his nose. Tateh was thin and stooped. His face was always creased with worry and wire-rimmed glasses magnified his dark eyes. His thin hair retreated further and further as if it had lost the battle with his furrowed forehead. But when you saw the two brothers together, you knew they loved each other.

Bubbe usually stayed in her room only joining us for meals. She was too old to leave the apartment. The climb up and down four flights of stairs was too much for her and mamah said she was too brokenhearted to leave her bedroom since her son had abandoned his faith. Bubbe hung a mezuzah on the inside of her bedroom door since tateh would not allow one to be nailed in the front hall. He believed men should not depend on religion for justice but join unions and demand fair treatment. In the evening, Uncle Avrom argued with him, but in such a light-hearted manner that it didn't seem as if the two brothers were actually quarreling. Mamah said that's what made Uncle Avrom such a good salesman.

That day I was in a real hurry to finish the potatoes. A new neighbor was moving in downstairs and I had overheard mamah say, "That Feldman is *mishugener*, since his wife died, totally *mishugener*." I had never heard mamah call anyone crazy, let alone two times in one sentence. Rachel replied, "Well, you know that girl played the piano even when her mother was alive." Mamah sniffed and whispered her answer.

I was eager to go outside to tell Mike and Izzy that our new neighbor, Feldman, was crazy. We had planned to watch him move in and already knew he had a daughter named Rebecca who played the piano. Feldman hired Tishman Brothers Movers to get the instrument into the third-floor apartment. Mamah called it a "grand piano" and laughed that it could not fit through the right angles in the narrow entry hall. The Tishmans were taking out the front window and raising the piano with ropes and pulleys to swing it into the apartment below us. The possibilities for an accident were great and my friends and I were meeting on the sidewalk to watch and to hope. When I was finally free of the kitchen, I ran out front. The piano was already in the air swaying back and forth, its giant keys grinning down at me like a monster's teeth.

I'd seen pictures of pianos and knew they had keys like an accordion but I never realized a piano's size or the beauty of its polished wooden curves. I was familiar with some musical instruments: the accordion, the fiddle, the harmonica that Uncle Avrom played. I had even hopped up and down to klezmer bands at weddings ,but I'd never seen or heard a real piano. Izzy, Mike and I watched as the Tishman brothers heaved and sweated to lift it to the third-floor window. Feldman was there with his daughter, Rebecca. He was a slight, nervous man who kept tugging at the scarf around his neck. Rebecca stood still and stared up in the air. Her arms and legs were as thin as a grasshopper's and, I thought, when summer ended and school began that would be her nickname. I noticed her top teeth protruded a little, resting on her lower lip. I always sucked my lower lip when doing arithmetic. The columns of numbers never made sense and I would chew on my lip in frustration as I tried to decipher them. I assumed Rebecca lacked the strength to tackle that giant instrument swinging above us and she had to chew her lower lip with the effort. I soon found out how wrong I was.

I heard a piano for the first time that night. A deep sound rose up from the floorboards, like the growl of a wild animal, and shook the thin metal legs of my cot. I had been sitting there picking the scab on my knee and the reverberation made me stop and hold my breath. It was followed by a long warble that rose higher and higher and ended just short of a screech. Rachel was passing by and huffed, "Well, I hope we don't have to listen to that noise every day or I'll have to lock myself in the room with bubbe." I leaned back against the wall and, from that moment, the sound captivated me. We soon learned that Rebecca played the piano three and sometimes four hours a day. With the windows open, the music floated in as well as rose up from the floor. I began to sit on my cot as the notes poured through the air. It was as if I were mesmerized and could not hear enough of the music.

That summer, as each day passed, I spent more and more time indoors listening to Rebecca play. I stopped rushing through my chores since I no longer planned to meet Izzy and Mike in the alley behind the shoe shop Izzy's father owned. Mr. Pearlman was a renowned shoemaker and he made shoes for many of the fashionable ladies on the Gold Cost. Izzy was blessed—or cursed—with small, narrow feet. Many of the women would pay Mr. Pearlman twenty-five cents extra if their leather shoes were softened, stretched, slightly worn in. That was Izzy's job. He would scrub his feet, encase them in gauze stockings and slip on a pair of fancy ladies' shoes. Then he walked round and round, like a dog chasing his own tail, on a raised wooden platform in the alley behind the shop. The platform was covered with a clean carpet and, when Mr. Pearlman brought the carpet out to the yard, we all knew Izzy would have to go to work. Mike and I never teased him; we only felt embarrassment and pity for him. In my heart, I knew his job was worse than any kitchen work. Once he finished and freed himself from the shoes, Izzy would break loose like a wild man and cause more mischief than Mike and I combined.

We never visited each other's houses, but just met in the alley. When I stopped showing up, I'm not sure what they thought. However, mamah began to worry about me and would come into the parlor to feel my forehead or bring me cool tea. "Nu, is the heat bothering you?" She'd ask. "Are you feeling not well?" I began to hold an open arithmetic book on my lap so I could tell her I was studying and wanted to do well in school this year. It was the one subject I hated and I always got the lowest grade in class. Mamah only looked at me and nodded.

As I listened to the music I soon learned there was an order to the pieces Rebecca played. I didn't know the titles or the composers but, after a few months, I knew the melodies and the images they brought to my mind. There was a melancholy piece filled with lamentations and a spritely one with the sound of galloping horses' hooves and chatter of sparrows skirmishing over bread crumbs. There were slow dreamy pieces that reminded me of the union picnic in the park last year. I had left my friends to sit under a tree and stare at the vast expanse of water. It was how I imagined the ocean. I had eaten too much, played too hard, and sat tired and drowsy on the soft grass. There were distant voices and laughter, the whir of chirping crickets. The wind caressed the trees, the waves lapped on Lake Michigan's shore and, with my eyes closed, I listened to the unfamiliar sounds of nature. The music downstairs mimicked these sounds and brought back sweet memories of that day.

Rebecca always finished by playing the same powerful piece. The music started with light, quick notes as her fingers scurried across the keys. The notes became louder, darkly dramatic until the swell of sound exploded and, at its peak, felt as if it would break through the floor. Rebecca's music showed me a measure of beauty in the world I barely knew existed. I waited for that powerful piece each evening, both enchanted by it and melancholy as it signified an end for the night.

In late winter I learned that a true end was near. At supper one night mamah said, "Feldman is getting married to the widow Herschel. Can you believe it? But, I guess, a child needs a mother."

"I heard at the factory that they are moving to a fancy apartment uptown," Rachel said.

"What! Why would they have to move?" I was shocked.

"Ester Herschel isn't going to live in this run-down building," Rachel answered.

"But Rebecca's fine. She doesn't need a mother," I insisted.

Mamah shook her head. "A man cannot raise a child alone and we all know only a mother's heart can understand what a child fails to say." I was confused by mamah's words, but the conversation had already shifted to the strike looming at the steel mills. I realized my music would be gone and began to spend every free moment with my ear glued to the floor so I could learn the melodies and never forget them.

The move happened on a warm day in early spring. The Tishman brothers came again and reversed the process to extract the piano. I did not go and watch, but sat limp on my cot and felt as if a part of me had died. I spent a lot of that summer indoors, reading and studying. Izzy and Mike had made friends with the Schneider twins and I was no longer a member of the gang. My grades improved and teachers began to talk to me about "going on in school." Rachel teased me that, all of a sudden, I was a scholar. Tateh was puzzled and kept asking when I would go to work. Uncle Avrom was hurt that I didn't want to help him. But I knew I couldn't work in the packing house like tateh or peddle dry goods like Uncle Avrom. I wasn't sure what I would do but I realized there was a greater world calling me away from the neighborhood. Mamah never questioned my dedication but made sure I had time to study and brought me small treats—an apple, a rugelach she had baked—as I poured over my books. I wonder if, indeed, she had known the secrets of my heart before I ever understood them, before I taught others to open their hearts and listen to music with passion and wonder.

I never discovered what became of Rebecca. Recently, I searched her name on the Internet but I didn't know if she had married. The name "Rebecca Feldman" brought up no one who matched her age and played the piano. I would have liked to tell her how much her music changed my life. Now, when I hear Chopin's "Heroic Polonaise," I can see my young self. My ear is pressed to the floorboards and the smells of old wax and vermin dust fill my nostrils. The music rises around me in waves, covers me and sends shivers down my back as it nudges me forward into my future.

Final Night of Hanukkah

Janet Spangler

he is old
his teeth are going
he is eating applesauce on the final night of Hanukkah
the joy is in its crust of sugar

he fumbled with the match but, at last,
Shabbos candle in his hand
lit the candles right to left
recited the blessings
came out strong on the *oh-h-mein*
performed the ritual

the family sees the candles doubled,
reflected in the night window

breaking out in Yiddish
they begin to sing the old songs

when the last candle sputters, disappears
they do not notice

summer's turn

for Jade

Ingrid Swanberg

I toil now,
below humming bees
the loud castanets of cicadae
and the gentle shadows
of monarch and swallowtail,
near where
you are newly lain
under the earth
beside the rare white violet
that blooms all summer long.

the quiet here builds into a wind
no less quiet for all the rasp of silk
as it enters the canopy.

only a few days past
I found a leaf,
the first one down
from the oak

but I did not then
understand
what it spoke,

green and rose and brown.

Small News Item in the Midst of War

Francine Marie Tolf

It could be chance that out of
our own darkness
and the world's,
out of sleep
and that hour before dawn,
the first sound we hear,
if we are lucky enough
to live where it makes its home,
is the liquid questioning of a bird,
testing the day's reality with her song.

And maybe the bubbles that cluster
like clear beads on stems in vases
are chance too, and the elaborate feathers
of ice that form on windows in winter.
Beauty could be an accident.

So I must not make too much
of the bird I read about
who built her nest from the scrap
of detonated land mines:

who absolves, every morning,
the dark of a greenless field
with notes that sound beautiful.

⋮

136

⋮

Picking Your Partner (excerpted from a larger article)

Brian Treglown

It's great to be talented, especially if you are going to make a career entertaining others. If you don't happen to be talented, not to worry. You can still become famous and live a prosperous life. What you need to do is pick a partner who is talented—after all, one of you has to be. Then be very nice to your partner and hope that he or she will carry you along for the ride. Here are some guys who seem to have done just that.

<u>Simon and Garfunkel</u>—I have always loved the singing duo Simon and Garfunkel. Their hits "Sound of Silence," "Parsley, Sage, Rosemary, and Thyme," and "Bridge Over Troubled Water" were wonderful pop songs. They were the premiere male duet singers from the '60s and '70s. Eventually they went their separate ways, and Paul Simon established himself as a famous singer-songwriter, one of popular music's most successful.

But Art Garfunkel? Well, not so much. He had a sweet, high tenor voice, which worked fine with Simon's slightly lower tenor. But all their songs were written by Simon. I bought an album by Garfunkel released a few years after his breakup with Simon. To be honest, it was dreadful. All the songs seemed to be retreads of songs others had done. And they were just kind of thrown together; occasionally the backgrounds got terribly out of tune.

The problem was clear. As long as Simon's songwriting skills produced great material, the Simon and Garfunkel songbook was great. But without Simon, Garfunkel had little to go on. He's never regained the success the two of them had. Garfunkel basically did one thing right. He picked Paul Simon as his singing partner. Good move. I'm hoping he invested his royalties well.

<u>Hall and Oates</u>—Hall and Oates were one of rock music's most successful duos. The two guys met at Temple University in

Philadelphia. Over the life of their career, they produced twenty-one albums, and had ten #1 hit songs. It's a significant achievement.

But listen to their songs. You can readily hear Daryl Hall's powerful voice belting it out. But you don't hear Oates. I guess on occasion he provides some back-up singing. And he plays guitar on all their hits. But let's be honest—guitar players in the '60s and '70s were plentiful. You just have to presume that Daryl Hall's strong voice carried Oates along to stardom. Like Art Garfunkel, I think John Oates got incredibly lucky, teaming up with a very talented singer.

Once the guys broke up, we never heard much again from John Oates. He's still around, still produces a few albums of other singers. But of his own material? Nope.

Brooks and Dunn—The story of Brooks and Dunn is an interesting one. In country music the conventional wisdom is that there is room for maybe one successful duo act at a time. And in the '80s that act was The Judds. They were a mother and daughter duo, and they had a long string of country hits. But in the '80s, Naomi Judd, the mother, contracted hepatitis, and went into retirement.

So record producer Don Cook wondered if he could come up with a replacement for The Judds. He had two singers under contract, one from Oklahoma, one from Louisiana, who hadn't been able to come up with a hit. They didn't know each other, but Cook got Kix Brooks and Ronnie Dunn in a studio together, and they recorded "Brand New Man," which turned out to be a hit. Fine.

Reluctantly, they agreed to record a follow-up song. Cook chose a song called "Boot Scootin' Boogie" for that. Turns out there was a new line dance that went with "Boot Scootin' Boogie," and this song, intended only as a follow-up to the first hit, became what they call a "monster hit." Country record of the year, wildly popular line dance, and all that. Based on the success of the follow-up song, there was no way that Brooks and Dunn could walk away from each other. Like it or not, they were a duo. And a long string of hits followed.

Solitary Vireo

Claudia Van Gerven

Not so much a bird
as a sound, yet not
so much a sound
as memory from the cool, leafy heart
of a tree
we want to believe
we remember

the fallacy so pathetic
but infallible still—
that a note wrested
from that locus
of reptilian blood
and hollow bone mingled
with polished amber
floors of old libraries
and the feel of
thumbed books, the heavy pleasure
of summer rain,
and a terse flash
of feathers—

whatever business, libidinous
or combative the bird
meant by it—

should so accurately state
the fierce stammering
beneath the poems
we cannot write.

"Claire de Lune"
Dianalee Velie

The rootless winds wrestled
twisting trees outside
the Shrewsbury Community Church,
bellowing along with the old piano
to the strains of "Claire de Lune."

The late afternoon sky, placating fall,
acquiesced to a gallery of grays
and intensifying shadows,
preparing evening's palette,

when the young pianist rested
his hands on the keyboard
and closed his eyes. The last note
resonated, drifted through the chapel,

and hung in the rafters before
orbiting outdoors, where the leaves,
tornadoing into clusters, stood still.
Captivated by the imminent silence

following the last clear note,
the wind wound down, the pianist
paused, the audience pondered,
everyone entering Debussy's dream,

until the full moon rose with thundering
applause, illuminating the dormant
darkness with the consenting clarity
of a single shimmering tone.

Orphean Aria
Dianalee Velie

Like a prayer, my Sunday litany
of tomatoes, garlic, and onion
simmers on the stove while
Puccini's aria, "Un Bel Di,"
rises to heaven with the aroma
and steam of draining pasta.

The misty kitchen window weeps
pious tears as outside a sudden
November snow squall
laces the night sky with holiness,
settling on the earth like dust
on an unopened family bible.

Your hunger now obvious,
you uncork the wine,
kiss the nape of my neck,
and seize the warm bread from the oven.
My blush surges with your blood
and the operatic voices

as we compose our own Orphean aria,
a domestic passion play, Bacchus once again
seducing Vesta's willing handmaiden,
befittingly before the hearth.

Music in the Air: Sounding the Waters

Elaine Wagner

It's summer in the park; I struggle to compose a melody
for my latest poem. Flying notes zip past me – I grab one,
then another. A dotted quarter and paired eighth notes
elude my grasp, weave round my arms, force me to wave,
                                                    flutter, rise in the air,
propel me toward a large oak tree.
"No!" I scream. Notes dart from my mouth like hornets,
seize my clothes, hair, carry me over the tree, then
drop me splash! into a pond.
Blue staccato notes jump from the water, ping the air,
startle several passersby.
My feet push up from mud,
my head breaks the surface with cymbals clash,
I gasp, fill my lungs with air, exhale
transparent whole notes which
float over the pond like soap bubbles.
Sunlight on water chimes sapphire-diamonds,
some rays penetrate the surface, dart presto! like tiny fish,
send sonar rippling under water,
then rise basso profundo in the air as heat waves.
I swim toward shore, each splashing stroke sprays crashing droplets;
drag myself adagio up muddy banks, through cattails and tall grass.
Every stalk I touch during this amphibious
return twangs old-time country blues.
Back on land, I've found more than a melody—
I've unleashed a symphony with mud-squelching footsteps the finale.

Performances

J. Weintraub

Although she was hidden, obscured from view,
and I saw none of her dance,
I rise with the others as if I, too,
had been enlightened, entranced,
joining them in their feverish applause,
homage to a grace unseen—because
at that same moment, across the world,
a musician touches his head to the ground
as the tingling, glittering, vibrating sound
of his gong trembles into the trill
and silence of the dense tropic air;
and Lear rehearses his tragic lines,
collapsing into death over fair
Cordelia, and for the hundredth time
brings tears to his daughter's eyes;
and a young girl, alone, her last run before night,
skims over a field of ice,
and with blades flashing in the sun's lowering light,
she gathers speed, bends poised, then leaps,
spins once—still ascending—twice,
and up to heights she'll never reach
again, defying all natural law,
a third time, before she descends
on point, spinning slow to an end,
her arms outstretched, awaiting our applause.

The Buddha's Old Flute

Anthony White

At my lips since birth,
invisible,
the Buddha's stout old
bamboo flute.

The Buddha breathes hiss
weet, cool, jasmine,
Yin melodies
into my eager lips.

Then I breathe my
pungent, musky, wet,
Yang music
into the Buddha.

Let these harmonies
lead the joyous dance;
do not pull away
the old flute just yet.

Mandolin

Anthony White

When I came into this world, the master mandolin maker
gave me a fine instrument in a fitted black case.
I have never seen it, but sometimes—
when I hear certain music—
there is a vibration inside me.
Now the case is old and worn.
Soon I will open the case and take the gift home.

Today I Wanted to Write about Plants

Paula Yup

Only to write about being homesick
with such a yearning
that there was no room for cholla,
candelabra, old man, organ pipe,
pitaya agria, yucca, Palo Adan,
ocotillo, elephant tree, mesquite,
Mammalaria, boojum, limberbush,
creosote bush, ironwood, smoke tree,
jojoba or cardon in my thoughts.
Masybe manana will be the day for plants
to sing their sweet songs to me
soothing me calming me in this desert place.

Greatest Hits

Peggy Zabicki

Stuck on You
High on You
Thoughts of You
You're in My Heart
My Heart Belongs to You
You Broke My Heart
You Still Have My Heart
Fix My Broken Heart
Let's Fix This Thing
We've Got a Good Thing
We've Got Each Other
Two Hearts
My Heart Aches for You
Fix My Broken Heart and the Bathroom Sink
I've Got a Sinking Feeling
Feeling Lonely
Where Were You Last Night?
A Six Pack of Excuses
Forgive and Forget
We've Come This Far
All I Need Is the Beer on Your Breath
We're Stuck with Each Other

Uncle Marlyn's Banjo

Marilyn Zelke-Windau

When you painted the palm trees
on the skin of the banjo,
did you wish for tropics?
Or did you wish for away?
When you serenaded
doorways, window leanings
on four-string summer evenings,
did you pluck
skinny schoolgirl hearts
or firm-formed, farm-girl flesh?
Did the moon illumine
the roadway leading out of town?
Or did it scare you enough
to revise another tune of stay?
When the money got good,
without schooling,
and the pigs you raised
penned assets of ham,
did you forget
the sailing boat,
blue-gliding its way
from Fremont,
with good tidings?
Did you settle for clay in your boots
instead of light sand?
Did you ever dust the wires
with melody dreams again?

Thrust

Marilyn Zelke-Windau

Brazilian music beckons.
My toes twitch,
calves cramp.
My thighs feel blood descending,
ascending to core,
and I dance
as though I belong
to the Portuguese,
to the south,
to the opposite swirl of water
down pipes in this
northern hemisphere of Wisconsin.
The music becomes me
and I the music
as water reaches,
water branches,
thrust so many miles,
so many lifetimes past,
to find me
dancing.

$\vdots$

147

$\vdots$

GORAN COBAN SALON

For my father

who fed my love of books
by driving me to the public library
on jasmine-scented Los Angeles evenings

BARBARA CRANE

Congratulations

To my fellow anthology contributors;
especially to Grace Kuikman and William Grady
whose stories entertain me twice a month
and...
Margaret Lisle, who has been a most supportive friend.

A very special thanks to

Whitney Scott

whose hard work for the TallGrass Writers Guild,
and as editor of these acclaimed anthologies
makes all this possible.

Nighttime's Glory

Sitting in the nighttime's glory
the moon and stars tell their stories,
staring at the moonlit sky.
The sun rose. I said goodbye.

Samantha "Sam" Dodd was ten years old when she composed this poem, one of many she wrote to help her deal with the trauma of her father's terminal brain cancer. Sam's creativity and fortitude are a reminder that no matter the age or inspiration of the writer, their words spring from the deepest wellings of the heart.

How would your life be different if just one thing changed?

A Matter of Happenstance

A four-generation family saga novel

By

Catherine Underhill Fitzpatrick

Best wishes to Outrider Press
and
TallGrass Writers Guild

Maggie Reister Walters
CLU, ChFC, CLTC

522 E 86th Ave.
Merrillville, IN, 46410
219.756.3849
Fax: 219.756.4103
Cell: 219.308.0137

mareister@financialguide.com

TallGrass Writers Guild

TallGrass Writers Guild is open to all who write seriously at any level. The Guild supports members by providing performance and publication opportunities via its multi-page, bi-monthly newsletter, open mics, formal readings, annual anthologies, and the TallGrass Writers Guild Performance Ensemble programs. In affiliation with Outrider Press, TallGrass produces its annual "Black-and-White" anthologies, the results of international calls for themed contest entries. Cash prizes and certificates awarded result from the decisions of independent judges. The Guild is a rarity among arts organizations in that it has been and remains largely self-sufficient despite the challenges facing non-profit arts organizations. For more information on TallGrass Writers Guild membership and programs, call 219-322-7270 or telephone toll-free at 1-866-510-6735. Email tallgrassguild@sbcglobal.net .

The Judge

Diane ("Diva Di") Williams, author of *Performing Seals*, is a prize-winning poet and essayist who has a novel in progress. A graduate of Chicago's Columbia College, "Judge Diva" was awarded a literary fellowship that took her to Ireland for extensive study. She lives and writes in Chicago, and teaches at Kendall College.

The Editor

Whitney Scott plays many roles in Chicago's literary scene. She is an author, editor, book designer and reviewer whose poetry, fiction and creative nonfiction have been published internationally, earning her listings in *Contemporary Authors* and *Directory of American Poets and Fiction Writers*. A member of the Society of Midland Authors, she performs her work at colleges, universities, arts festivals and literary venues throughout the Chicago area and has been featured as guest author in the Illinois Authors Series at Chicago's Harold Washington Library. Scott was awarded the 2009-10 Writer-in-Residence Award from Bensenville Public Library, is judge of the 2010 National Federation of Press Women writing competition, and regularly reviews books for the American Library Association's *Booklist* magazine.

To Order
Outrider Press Publications
effective January 1 2006, all prices include applicable taxes

____Music in the Air–$21   _____
Symphonies, Pop, Rock, Nature's birdsong
____Deep Waters–$21   _____
Rivers, lakes, naval warfare, emotional depths
____A Bird in the Hand: Risk and Flight–$21   _____
Casinos, runaway teens, and birds, birds, birds
____Seasons of Change– $21   _____
The natural world, technology, personal identity
____Fearsome Fascinations–$21   _____
Bad boys, vamps, werewolves, forbidden fruit
____Wild Things–Domestic and Otherwise   _____
bats, rivers, children running wild
____A Walk Through My Garden–$21   _____
crocuses, digital gardening, farms, flowerpots
____Vacations–$20   _____
From stolen moments to Roman holidays
____Falling in Love Again–$20   _____
Love the second time around
____Family Gatherings–$20   _____
Weddings, wakes, holidays and more
____Take Two–They're Small –$20   _____
Food, food, food
____A Kiss is Still a Kiss–$19   _____
Romantic love
____Earth Beneath, Sky Beyond–$19   _____
Nature and our planet
____Feathers, Fins & Fur–$18   _____
Animals
____Freedom's Just Another Word–$17   _____
What is freedom?
____Alternatives: Roads Less Travelled–$17   _____
Night shifts, new directions, the counter-culture
____Prairie Hearts–$17   _____
Writings on the Heartland

Add s/h charges:
$3.95 for 1 book...$6.95 for 2 books...$2.50 each add'l   _____

                          TOTAL   _____

Outrider Press
2036 N. Winds Drive
Dyer, IN 46311